The
Deep End

OTHER BOOKS BY
TRACI HUNTER ABRAMSON:

Undercurrents

Ripple Effect

The Deep End

a novel

Traci Hunter Abramson

Covenant Communications, Inc.

Cover Image: © BananaStock / Alamy

Cover design copyrighted 2007 by Covenant Communications, Inc.

Published by Covenant Communications, Inc.
American Fork, Utah

Printed in the United States of America
First Printing: August 2007

11 10 09 08 07   10 9 8 7 6 5 4 3 2 1

ISBN 978-1-59811-199-6

ACKNOWLEDGEMENTS

Thank you to my husband, Jonathan, for supporting my dreams. Thanks to my daughters Diana, Christina, and Lara for sharing me with the computer, and to my son Luke for taking long naps.

My continued thanks to Rebecca Cummings for reading everything I write and making it better, and to Mandy Abramson for liking everything I write even when it's only a rough draft.

As always, thank you to the wonderful people at Covenant who help bring out the best in what I write, especially Angela Eschler and Kathryn Jenkins.

My sincere thanks to Laura Cwick for sharing her invaluable knowledge of elite swimming.

Finally, thank you to all of my friends and readers who asked, "What happened next?"

To my swimmers, who inspire me,
and to my family for sharing me with them.

PROLOGUE

Jimmy Malloy leaned back in his lounge chair and flipped through the morning *New York Times*. He didn't give a thought to the expense of obtaining the paper each morning on the little desert island of Bonaire. He wanted it, so he got it. Simplistic, maybe, but that was how Malloy ran his house and his business. And it was his business now, even though Chris Rush still considered it his own.

Malloy often thought of his situation as poetic justice— the fact that his actions had ultimately caused the demise of his former employer. When two of his men had killed a cop and left a witness alive to testify, the entire smuggling organization headed by Rush had been jeopardized. Rush had been too arrogant to believe himself vulnerable, unwilling to give up his life as an apparently honorable federal judge until it was too late.

Malloy had been smarter than that. The house in Bonaire suited his purposes perfectly. The desert island was only fifty miles from Caracas and could be reached easily by plane or boat. When necessary, a man of his talents was capable of slipping past port authorities and entering Venezuela without leaving a paper trail. Once in the country, traveling from Venezuela to Colombia was hardly complicated with the network he had built over the past decade. After all, drugs would always turn a profit, and cocaine and its by-products had long been the lifeblood of the organization.

The sun was high in the sky as he glanced over the water at a speedboat heading out with a group of scuba divers. He was considering moving inside to escape the warm spring air when the patio door opened. Malloy looked up but didn't move as Miguel Artez approached him.

"Well?" Malloy left the unspoken question hanging in the air.

"They arrive in Aruba tonight." Miguel spoke in a quiet voice. "Everything is ready."

Malloy swung his long legs over the side of the lounge chair. "It will look like an accident?"

Miguel nodded. "No one will know."

"Inform me when it's over."

* * *

Tom Miller stepped onto the wooden dock and walked toward the speedboat that would take him off the coast of Aruba. White, sandy beaches stretched behind him, and the sun glistened off the water beyond. The beauty was wasted on Tom. He just wanted to get to where they were going.

Most of the tourists lingering on the dock had taken the scuba class that morning that was required for uncertified divers. Tom's all-expenses-paid trip to Aruba included the basic course along with a dive every afternoon with this particular scuba shop. He figured they were as good as any as long as he got to do an advanced dive.

Besides Tom, only one other person in the class had been scuba diving before. The two of them would go out on a more advanced dive, while the beginners in the class would take a second boat to an easier dive site. Tom thought it a bit odd that the other advanced diver, Larry, already seemed to know their instructor, but when Tom thought to ask about it, Larry explained that he vacationed in Aruba every year and remembered Bill from the year before.

The beginning dive group was already loading up in the second boat. Tom reached the spot where the air tanks were lined up waiting to be loaded. When he reached for a tank, Bill, the instructor, stopped him.

"Hold on a second. Let me make sure everyone gets the right one."

"Does it matter?" a woman with the beginning group asked before Tom thought to voice the question.

"Since most of you are using rented equipment, we just have to make sure you have what was signed out to you." Bill handed Tom his air tank and then proceeded to help everyone else check their equipment.

Tom accepted the tank that Bill gave him and stepped onto the boat to store his gear. He took his seat, wiping the sweat off his face with his towel before setting it beside him. Since his first vacation to the Bahamas nearly fifteen years ago, he had enjoyed scuba diving. The stress and nerves that always seemed to plague him at work and at home melted away when he went below the water's surface. The beauty on the ocean floor never failed to amaze him, and he was looking forward to finding that peace again.

For months he had gone to work each day, always wondering if this was the day they would find him. He wasn't exactly sure who "they" all were, but he knew they were out there. Jimmy Malloy was the only name and face he could recognize, except for Chris Rush, the former judge whom he would testify against in a few months.

The knowledge that he was one of two witnesses—not the sole witness himself—should have given Tom some comfort. After all, what was the point of killing him if the girl was still alive to testify? Still, he knew from experience how determined Rush was to see the other witness knocked off. If Rush's men found the girl, they could find Tom.

Tom hoped when the trial was over he would finally be able to relax. Maybe he would take his wife's advice more seriously and move their family to some tropical place where he could dive and where she and the kids could enjoy the outdoors. Surely he could find a new job and a new life for himself and his family. He wasn't sure which bureaucrat had chosen Boise, Idaho, for his new residence, but the only time he seemed to spend outside was when he had to shovel more snow off the driveway. As the winter months had dragged on, his wife's suggestion to relocate after the trial had grown more and more appealing.

This vacation had come at the perfect time, giving them a chance to get away from reality, or at least to have the illusion of escaping it. Even now his wife and kids were at the beach, probably lathering on sunscreen and playing in the sand. The thought flashed into his mind that he should have informed the FBI when he had won this free trip, but it was quickly pushed aside. After all, he deserved a little time off.

The feds didn't understand the constant pressure that came from pretending to be someone else all the time. They didn't know what it was like to see his wife and kids trying to adapt to a new city and a new home, all the while remembering that their last name was now Miller, not Abbott. As far as Tom was concerned, the FBI didn't *ever* need to know about this week away.

A spray of salt water misted over him as the boat pulled away from the dock and they headed out to sea. He glanced down at his dive watch, mildly annoyed that they were five minutes behind schedule. The boat bounced over the waves, and the sound of the engine made conversation with the other passengers difficult. Tom didn't mind; he didn't have much to say anyway.

Fifteen minutes later they arrived at Malmok Reef, the dive site. Tom began to strap on his equipment with ease and adjusted the diving weights in his belt that would help him counteract his natural buoyancy as he descended into the deep water.

Bill went over a few basic instructions before motioning to Tom. "Are you ready?"

Tom nodded. He took a last breath of sea air, put in his mouthpiece, and followed Bill beneath the surface. Dutifully, Tom checked his air gauge as they slowly descended. Giant barrel sponges colored the water orange, purple, and green. He continued deeper, two sting rays hovering nearby.

At nearly seventy feet below the surface, Tom moved toward some brain coral to study it more closely, unaware that Larry had circled around behind him. Again he checked his air gauge, for the first time realizing that it had not changed in the past twenty minutes. With the experience of a practiced diver, he turned to find Bill to signal that he was going back up to the surface. Though he was out of reach, Bill was close enough to see the signal.

Instead of signaling that he too would surface, Bill used his light to check the dive watch he wore. The warning that something wasn't quite right went off in Tom's head just a second before his air ran out. Panic showed in his eyes as he tried to move to Bill's position. He signaled with both hands that he didn't have any air.

When Bill moved away from him instead of toward him, Tom turned to look for help. Instead, he locked eyes with Larry. The man was clipping something onto Tom's diving belt and had tangled his equipment on the coral Tom had just been admiring. Tom held his breath as he struggled to free himself from his useless scuba equipment, but he continued to tangle in the lines that were clipped to his belt. He looked down to see the thick rope attached to an anchor just below them.

He watched Bill and Larry move away from him as he shed his air tank and tried once again to untangle himself. When finally he couldn't hold his breath any longer, he gasped, breathing in water instead of air. With one last surge of energy, Tom shed the rest of his equipment and started for the surface.

Excruciating pain filled his ears as he struggled upward. Logically, he knew that his body couldn't handle the rapid ascent, but panic and survival instinct took over. He even managed to delude himself that maybe he could survive after all, since the only pain was in his ears and sinuses rather than his chest. He held his breath, his head now throbbing as a tingling sensation crept along his skin. He thought of his wife and children alone on the beach and realized that maybe he should have told the FBI about this vacation after all. He was within fifteen feet of the surface when his struggles suddenly ceased, and he began drifting back down into the dark.

CHAPTER 1

CJ Whitmore stretched her arms high above her head, tucking her chin so that she was in a streamline position. Silently, she counted to ten before she let her body relax and then began stretching out the muscles in her arms. The swimming pool in front of her was now empty, the water rippling from the swimmers who had just finished their practice. A few teenagers still lingered on the deck, but CJ barely noticed them. Instead she studied the young woman stretching a few yards away.

At six feet tall, Bridget Bannon towered over CJ and possessed a confidence many athletes envied. She was the best female breaststroker in the world, and she knew it. For nearly a year, CJ had been training beside her. She would have liked to think of Bridget as a teammate, but CJ was more astute than that. They were two competitors striving for the same goal, and they just happened to share a coach.

CJ had only been with the team a few days when she was informed that the aquatics center where they practiced had been built to give Bridget a place to train. Her father had used his influence with the city government to have the state-of-the-art facility built when Bridget had started breaking swimming records at the age of thirteen.

Bridget had been just seventeen when she had made the Olympic team in the 200-meter breaststroke. Youth and inexperience had taken their toll on her, though, and she had not advanced beyond the semifinals in the event. Now, at twenty-one, expectations were high that she would finally bring home a medal to her family and the city of Philadelphia.

Focused on her goals, Bridget hadn't seemed to notice the addition of CJ to the elite team until just the week before. When their coach had lined them up for sprints, CJ had beaten Bridget in the 100-meter breaststroke for the first time. CJ had been thrilled, finally feeling like she was ready to compete with the world's best. Bridget's response had been disbelief, followed by a hard stare and a cold shoulder.

Their coach called out their warm-up, and CJ dove into an empty lane to begin. She glided through the water, finding comfort in the simple routine. By this time, a handful of other swimmers had entered the pool for their morning practice, most of them hoping for the same thing as CJ: a trip to the Olympics.

CJ finished her first warm-up set and again caught sight of Bridget. She thought of the way Bridget's mother often hovered over her after practices, despite the fact that Bridget was already an adult. She had seen situations like Bridget's before. Often athletes were so focused on their training that they remained dependent on their parents for everything, including making decisions. Though she understood how it could happen, CJ couldn't imagine living a life in which a parent was so controlling.

We're the same age, CJ thought to herself, struck by how different their lives were. Her own childhood had been idyllic, or at least as perfect as a child could have being raised by a widowed father. She had grown up knowing that she was loved by both her father and the members of her local church congregation—her ward. She thought back to the countless number of people from her church who had given her rides to swim practice, taught her to cook, and watched after her when her father was at work. She knew she would always be grateful that her father had raised her as a member of The Church of Jesus Christ of Latter-day Saints.

Her life's plans had been coming into focus after she graduated from high school, until her father's fatal heart attack had turned her world upside down. He had supported all of CJ's activities and interests, sacrificing so much to be there for her in everything she did. He had always told her she could do anything, and his death had cemented her resolve to prove him right. From that day forward, she had focused on making the Olympic team as much to fulfill her father's hopes as to pursue her own dreams.

Her closest friend, Chase, understood her motivation and encouraged her to use swimming as a way to work through the loss of her father. She had just begun focusing on her future again, one that would include attending Stanford on a swimming scholarship, when she had stopped by Chase's house one evening for a date they had planned.

That day had changed her life forever. Two men had charged into Chase's apartment, men that Chase knew through his work as a detective. Chase had been more concerned about her than he had been about himself, CJ realized now—he had sent her into his bedroom to protect her. Ultimately, CJ had escaped any harm the men would have inflicted on her, but Chase had died that day, just moments after uttering a warning that had taken her months to understand.

That had been almost three years ago, and the ordeal was almost over. The trial of Chris Rush, the man Chase had been investigating, would take place in June. CJ could hardly believe that she had been in the Witness Protection Program for so long, or that she had already assumed her third identity.

She wasn't sure how many times her location had been discovered by Rush, and she doubted that Doug Valdez, her agent in charge, would tell her how many times her life had been spared. She knew of at least four attempts on her life, two of which had resulted in her being relocated under a new name. After she finished testifying in June, she hoped to once again enjoy life outside the Witness Protection Program.

* * *

Matt Whitmore strolled down the street, passing the various bookstores and cafés along Rittenhouse Square in Philadelphia. With relief, Matt noticed the trees in full bloom, a sure sign of spring. Even though he had spent the last six weeks based out of Florida, he had been in Philly enough of the winter to be grateful that it was now behind him.

A boy about seven years of age tugged on Matt's sleeve, causing him to slow mid-stride. The request for his autograph caught him by surprise, even though he knew he should be used to it by now. Matt accepted the proffered piece of paper, signed it, and handed it back with a smile. The boy's face split into a huge grin, revealing a gap where a tooth should have been. The boy's mother thanked Matt before ushering her son back to the park.

As a young boy, Matt had fantasized about a career in baseball. However, as he grew into his teenage years, he had been practical enough to realize it would probably never happen. Now, in just his second season as a professional baseball player, he was already playing in the major leagues.

A woman sitting on a bench caught his attention. She was obviously pregnant, and Matt noticed a look of contentment on her face as she tossed a handful of breadcrumbs to the pigeons scurrying at her feet. Moments later, she smiled, her face radiating with joy as her husband came into view.

Matt watched them embrace before turning away. He wanted that in his own life, that sense of contentment, a family of his own. Just as those thoughts crossed his mind, he saw her. Slim and athletic, she moved through the crowded sidewalks with relative ease. Her dark hair was pulled back at the base of her neck, falling past her shoulders. Ivory skin stretched over high cheekbones, and her gray eyes surveyed the surroundings as she walked.

She hesitated ever so slightly when her gaze fell upon him. He stared a moment longer before forcing his eyes back to the sidewalk in front of him. His hands balled in frustration— here he was on a beautiful spring day, and he couldn't even acknowledge that he knew the dark-haired beauty down the street, much less the fact that he was married to her.

Always cautious when it came to his wife, Matt stopped in a bookstore and browsed for ten minutes before buying a magazine and heading for home. He lifted a hand in greeting to the doorman and crossed the plush lobby to the waiting elevator. He stepped inside, relieved to find it empty.

The doors slid open on the third floor, and Matt walked the short distance down the hall to his condominium. He stepped into the living room and disengaged the security system.

Thick, cream-colored carpet covered the spacious living room, as well as the hallway leading to the downstairs bedroom, which he had converted to a workout room. A serving bar separated the rarely used galley kitchen from the living area.

After locking the front door, Matt headed for the stairs leading to one of the master bedrooms. He ascended the curved staircase overlooking the two-story living area. He turned away from the master suite, instead turning to the wide hallway across from it. After having a second child, the previous owner had bought the condominium behind his, combining the two units into one.

The living arrangements perfectly suited Matt and CJ's needs. Matt always used the entrance on the third floor, as well as the address that went with it. The other condo was a single-level unit with an entrance on the fourth floor. CJ used that entrance to make it appear to the outside world that she and Matt lived on separate floors of the same building. In reality, they shared a three-bedroom condo that happened to include two kitchens and two living rooms.

Matt passed through the wide hall to where it joined the hallway by the master bedroom he shared with his wife. By the time he made his way into the living room, CJ was already in the kitchen fixing dinner. These moments were rare now that baseball season was underway. CJ was usually finished with her first practice of the day before Matt even got up in the morning. While CJ came to almost all of his games, she usually left early and was sound asleep by the time he got home. To protect her cover, they couldn't even attend church together.

Clinging to this little hint of normalcy, Matt grinned and walked into the kitchen. He slipped his arms around CJ's waist, gave her a kiss, and reached past her for a roll that was cooling on the counter.

CJ shook her head, trying not to laugh as he released her and tossed the hot bread from one hand to the other. "You're going to burn yourself one of these days."

"Nah." Matt leaned back against the counter as CJ picked up a bowl and mixed the ingredients of a pasta salad. "Something smells good."

"It's just roasted chicken. I figured you could eat the leftovers while I'm gone," CJ told him casually, but Matt recognized the sliver of fear just beneath the surface.

"You're really going to have to testify?" Matt asked, already knowing the answer.

"It looks that way."

"How long will you be gone?" Matt tried to keep his voice casual, but his underlying concern slipped through. He hated it when CJ had to testify, especially the fact that she needed protection and he couldn't be there to help keep her safe.

CJ shrugged. "Hopefully just a day or two."

"I wish I could go with you." Matt sighed, already anticipating all of the reasons he couldn't—mainly because they couldn't risk being seen together. "By the way, how did you get all of this done so fast? I just saw you outside fifteen minutes ago."

"I just ran down the block to pick up some milk." CJ glanced over her shoulder and shot him an accusing look. "Somehow the milk that was in the fridge this morning mysteriously vanished after I left for practice."

"Don't you hate it when that happens?" Matt teased, neither confirming nor denying his guilt. He thought of the couple he had seen in the park and let himself wish that he could enjoy simple moments like those with his wife outside of their condominium. Matt snatched another roll from the cooling rack, steam rising from the center of the bread when he broke it open. "You know, I'm getting really tired of pretending I don't know my own wife."

"It could be worse, you know."

"I know," Matt agreed reluctantly. He thought back to the day he had married her. He had chosen this, he thought now. He had walked into this marriage knowing full well that he would be married to a woman in the Witness Protection Program and that they would have to spend their first year of marriage pretending they didn't know each other. The fact that they were able to share living quarters was something of a minor miracle.

Just days before their wedding, Chris Rush, the man behind the many attempts on CJ's life, had discovered her false identity and sent her running for her life once again. Refusing to let Rush completely ruin their plans, they had secretly married in the Provo Temple, not knowing when they would be together again. Had Matt not been called up to the majors, they most certainly would have had to spend these past eight months apart. Matt's move to Philadelphia to play for the Phillies had allowed Witness Protection to relocate her to the condo adjoining his.

The timer on the stove buzzed, and CJ slipped an oven mitt on her hand to pull the chicken from the oven. "Did you get to play today?"

"A couple of innings at second," Matt shrugged. "I don't think the club knows what to do with me now that Henderson is healthy again and is doing fine at first base."

"Everything will work out," CJ stated as though speaking the words would make them come true. She set the chicken on the table and sat down.

"My baseball career is the least of my concerns right now." Matt just stared at her for a moment, tucking away her image so that he could remember it on the days when they couldn't be together. Finally, he picked up the bowl of pasta salad and set it on the table.

CJ watched him sit down and waited for his eyes to meet hers before she spoke. "Don't worry. I'm sure Doug has already checked everything out at least sixteen times to make sure I'll be safe."

Matt reached across the table and gave her hand a squeeze. "I'm counting on it."

CHAPTER 2

Doug Valdez walked through Denver International Airport, a scowl on his face. At midnight, the airport was sparsely populated, but Doug couldn't quite muster up the energy to be grateful for the lack of pedestrian traffic after spending three hours sitting on a runway in Dallas waiting to take off. He stepped onto an escalator, shifted his overnight bag, and dug his cell phone out of the pocket of his suit jacket. He didn't want to think about the fact that he had just picked up this suit from the dry cleaners the day before. Now it was as rumpled as he felt.

Doug followed the signs to ground transportation, hopeful that he could find a cab since he doubted the car rental agency was still open. Annoyed that he had been incommunicado for several hours more than expected, he flipped open his cell phone and scrolled through the first six messages. Three were from fellow FBI agents, two were from U.S. Marshals, and one was from CJ Whitmore. He checked the message from CJ first, relieved that her arrival for the trial in Denver had gone without incident.

After spending more than two of his seven years with the FBI working on CJ's case, Doug had learned to not only expect the unexpected, but to expect trouble every time CJ was around.

He walked past the car rental agency, frustrated that it was indeed closed. Moving toward an exit, he checked the rest of his phone messages. The anxiety that had been building in him over the past few hours eased as each subsequent message confirmed that no suspicious activity had been observed surrounding CJ's transport and accommodations.

Surprised to easily find a taxi, Doug climbed in the back-seat and gave the hotel name and address to the driver. He leaned his head back, giving in to the fatigue that always plagued him before a trial. Juggling a hundred details to ensure CJ's safety each time she testified was just part of the job. Admittedly, handling details was his strong point. He rubbed at his eyes, thinking how much smoother CJ's transportation and security had been for this trial compared to the previous trials in which she had testified.

Even as he thought of the bed waiting for him at the hotel, on another level of consciousness he analyzed what had been done differently to allow everything to go so smoothly. He couldn't remember the last time that CJ had testified when at least one problem hadn't occurred, whether it was a leak regarding her accommodations or a blatant threat against her life.

Details, Doug thought to himself. *Concentrate on the details.* The players had remained basically the same over the past several trials. The U.S. Marshals assigned to protect her were carefully screened, and each of them had been assigned to CJ before. No one else in the FBI had complete access to her file except for Keith Toblin. Keith had been reassigned to Baltimore specifically so that he would be close enough to oversee any problems that might arise while CJ was living in Philadelphia.

Doug had handled the travel orders and hotel reservations himself to minimize the number of people involved with the case. Since his transfer to the Miami office nearly three months before, he had officially been taken off the Rush case. Only a few key government officials knew that he was still in charge of CJ Whitmore's safety.

Doug had been working toward the transfer to Miami and the promotion that went with it for some time; he just wished it hadn't come before his wedding. Now he and his fiancée, Jill, often had to settle for long phone calls and a rare weekend together. It was one of those infrequent visits that had caused him to get stuck at the Dallas airport in the first place.

When the taxi pulled up in front of the hotel, Doug paid the driver and headed straight for the front desk.

"Good morning, sir," the desk clerk greeted him. On his shirt was a name tag that identified him as Michael Tacket, Night Manager. "Do you have a reservation?"

"Yes. Doug Valdez."

The manager punched a few buttons on his computer and retrieved a pass key. "Here it is. You will be in room 418. It looks like the rest of your party has already checked in."

Doug's face paled. Though he had made all of the hotel reservations, he had done each one separately so that they would not be connected. "Excuse me? When I made this reservation, I only reserved one room."

"Really?" Michael finished coding the key, slid it into an envelope, and set it on the counter before tapping a button on the keyboard again. "I have here that your agency reserved seven rooms for tonight. The other six occupants came in around the same time this evening."

Doug's heartbeat accelerated. Indeed, he had made reservations for six other people besides himself: Keith Toblin, CJ, and the four U.S. Marshals assigned to protect her. Yet Doug had used seven separate travel orders, paid with seven different credit cards, and made seven different phone calls. How had they been connected?

"I don't understand this," Doug mumbled, half to himself. He picked up his key, his mind whirling. "Why did you assume that all of these rooms are together?"

Michael turned the computer screen so Doug could see it. "When we take the reservation, we key in the travel order number. Our system can identify which agency the travel order originates from based on its number and then it assumes that all similar travel orders are linked together." Michael tapped the screen to show Doug where the travel order had been entered. "See how the first three characters are the same? The system just assumes they are all together and links them."

"Whose name would they be listed under?"

"Whoever checks in last." He continued to punch in numbers. "This will take just a minute. The system always gets confused when someone comes in after midnight."

"Whose name would it have been under before I got here?"

"The reservation is listed as incomplete until the last person in the group either checks in or cancels." The manager shrugged. "That's the one problem with this system. If someone calls looking for anyone in the party and doesn't know their room number, we can't access it unless we look through the registrations manually."

"Are you telling me that your system won't allow anyone to access the incomplete check-ins?"

"Basically, yes."

"In that case, how can I add one more person to this group?"

"If you do that, your reservations will stay open." The manager looked confused.

Doug could hardly tell him that he was trying to protect the identity of someone in the Witness Protection Program, so instead he relied on his acting abilities. Leaning in closer, he lowered his voice. "Look, one of the guys staying here is going through a really nasty divorce. His wife tracks him down wherever he goes and calls him all night long. She's just making his life miserable. Anyway, I really need him to focus on this seminar we came for. I would really appreciate it if you can add another reservation if that will help him get a good night's sleep."

"Well, I guess I can do that," Michael stated hesitantly, handing Doug a piece of paper. "You're going to have to pay for the empty room though."

"Fair enough." Doug filled out the reservation request, watching as Michael finally finished the reservation, then thanked Michael and turned toward the elevator. He took two steps before turning back. "Do all hotels use this kind of system?"

"It's not uncommon."

Doug shifted his overnight bag and nodded. "Thanks again for your help."

In his room three minutes later, Doug pulled out his cell phone and punched the speed dial for Keith Toblin's cell.

On the fifth ring, Keith finally picked up. "Toblin."

"Were you sleeping?"

"Does it matter?" Keith grumbled. "Please don't tell me that you called just to say you finally made it."

"Not exactly." Doug suppressed a grin. "What room are you in? I need to talk to you."

"I'm in 412."

Doug hung up as he left his room. A dozen steps later, he knocked on Toblin's door.

Keith yanked the door open, wearing only the pair of sweat pants he had obviously been sleeping in. Brown eyes glared at Doug from beneath dark blond hair. Doug noticed the shiny, red scar on Toblin's shoulder, a souvenir and constant reminder from the men who wanted CJ dead. Keith stepped back to let Doug inside as he pulled on a T-shirt. "This had better be good."

"I just had an interesting conversation with the night manager," Doug said, following Keith into the room.

"And?" Keith asked, still blurry eyed.

"You know how we kept having trouble with hotel security with CJ?"

"Yeah." Instinctively, Keith touched a hand to the old wound. "What about it?"

"I think I've figured out how Rush's men keep finding her." Doug leaned against the dresser and relayed the information he had gleaned from Michael.

"You think they've figured out how to monitor the hotel reservation system?" Keith reached for his weapon, which was lying on the bedside table.

Doug nodded. "Think about it. Just about every time she testifies, we have some kind of trouble at the hotel. If I hadn't come in late, they probably would have already identified where we're staying."

"Maybe we should make a reservation somewhere across town. You know, let them think we are somewhere else."

"That's not a bad idea." Doug pushed away from the dresser and took a step toward the door. "I'll get one of the marshals to come with me to check in somewhere else. In the meantime, call the prosecuting attorney. Let him know that CJ has to testify first thing in the morning. If we can move up her testimony, we should be able to get her out of here before Rush's men figure out what's going on."

"I'll take care of it," Keith assured him.

* * *

CJ stepped down from the witness stand as two U.S. Marshals stepped forward to escort her out of the courtroom.

She blinked back the tears that threatened, trying to turn her mind away from the events that had changed her life forever. Each time she testified, she was reminded of how quickly she had lost everyone close to her. First her father, then just a month later the first man she had ever loved. Now she was determined that Chase's death would not be in vain. Others in law enforcement had tried and failed to penetrate Rush's organization. Chase had succeeded, and it had cost him his life.

Each time CJ testified it was the same thing: a detailed explanation of how she had identified Chris Rush as the head of the smuggling organization. The words Chase had spoken just before his death had been the key: *Chris . . . Rush . . . Don't let him find you.* At first she had taken the word "Chris" as the nickname Chase had often used for her. Months later, Matt had introduced her to Judge Christopher Rush, and CJ realized that with Chase's dying breath, he had tried to warn her about Rush.

Though she hadn't remembered it until she had figured out Chase's message, she had also seen a list of names when she had wandered through Chase's apartment before he was killed. The names had been arranged in an organizational chart. At the top was the name Christopher Rush. She found out later that Chase had been waiting for one of the other detectives he worked with to come by and pick up the evidence he had collected. Unfortunately, Rush's men had gotten there first.

Shaking her head clear of such images, CJ took a deep breath, wondering, waiting. She knew this trial was a test in more ways than one. Though the man on trial was charged with seemingly minor crimes compared to those committed by many in Rush's smuggling organization, he had refused to plea bargain, forcing CJ to take the stand once again. This was also the last trial she would testify in before Rush would finally stand before a judge.

Security had been unbelievably tight when she had first arrived, to the point that she had been practically invisible when she got to the courthouse two hours before the building even opened. She had entered with Doug Valdez and Keith Toblin, all three disguised in security guards' uniforms. With her hair tucked up in a cap, she doubted she even looked like a woman from a distance.

She certainly couldn't complain that Doug had managed to move her testimony up a day, but she always got nervous when her schedule changed suddenly. She took another deep breath. Now she could only pray that her departure from the courthouse would go as smoothly as her arrival.

One of the marshals took her by the arm and led her through a side doorway. Doug and Keith met them in the hallway and escorted her to a nearby exit. Her eyes darted down the hallway, and a sigh of relief escaped her when she saw that the corridor was empty.

She knew she should be used to the extra protection by now, especially since last year when an assassin had penetrated the already-tight security measures and nearly managed to silence her for good. Still, as the four armed men surrounded her, she could feel her heart pounding and wondered if this time one of Rush's men might succeed.

Months had passed since she had faced any viable threat, unless she considered driving during Philadelphia's rush hour dangerous. Still, when she had begged to be allowed to compete in the U.S. Nationals for swimming, Doug Valdez had shut her down. The FBI and the U.S. Marshals had been in complete agreement that a meet of that importance would be too great a risk for her.

CJ knew that the marshals were testing their security measures this week. If she could make it back to Philadelphia without incident, maybe they would let her try to qualify for the Olympic trials. The FBI and the U.S. Marshals had already approved the security plan for the swim meet the following weekend. It would be the first time she would be allowed to compete since moving to Philadelphia. Of course, those plans hinged on the success of this week's security measures.

She stepped outside, and bright sunlight blinded her momentarily. She heard the car approaching before she saw it, but the hand on her arm remained steady. Her free hand lifted to shade her eyes, and a sigh of relief escaped her when she saw that the car pulling up to the curb was driven by another U.S. Marshal. A second car, identical to the first, parked directly behind it. CJ was loaded into the first car along with Doug and one of the marshals. Keith and the other marshal got into the second car before both vehicles pulled away from the courthouse.

CJ closed her eyes, praying silently for safety. She didn't have to look out the window to know that the other car would veer off in another direction to create a viable decoy. Breathing deeply, she tried to relax as she put yet another trial behind her.

CHAPTER 3

CJ walked inside the condo, a smile crossing her face when she found Matt sitting in the kitchen reading the newspaper.

"Hey there!" Matt stood and crossed the room as CJ dropped her overnight bag on the floor. "I didn't expect to see you until tomorrow."

"The DA had me testify first thing this morning," CJ explained, reaching up to press her lips to his. The tension in her neck and shoulders eased as his arms came around her and pulled her close.

"I missed you." Matt skimmed his fingers along her jaw and studied her a moment. "Did everything go okay?"

"It was fine." CJ let out a sigh. "I'm just glad it's over."

"Me too." Matt took her hand and nodded toward the kitchen table. "Come sit down and eat something. You can tell me about it over breakfast."

"It's almost one o'clock," CJ pointed out, sitting down across from him. Taking a look at what he had chosen for breakfast, she shook her head, wondering if he would ever outgrow Lucky Charms. "What time do you have to leave for your game?"

"In a few minutes." Matt settled back into his chair and took a bite of his marshmallow-laden cereal. "By the way, thanks for leaving me that note about my car."

CJ grinned widely. Right before leaving for her trip, the mechanic working on Matt's car had called and left a voice mail saying that he could pick the car up anytime. Knowing that he wasn't likely to check for voice mails, she had left him a note in the one place he was guaranteed to find it: inside the cookie jar. "How long did it take you to find it?"

"Let's see." He tapped a finger to his lips. "I walked in from the game, kicked off my shoes, and went into the kitchen." Matt nodded as though recalling a distant memory. "It must have been two, maybe three minutes after I got home before I found it."

"You always have had a weakness for my chocolate-chip cookies." CJ laughed.

"Very true." Matt glanced at his watch and stood up. "I'd better get going."

CJ nodded, tipping her head back to kiss him good-bye. "Have a good game."

"See you later." Matt picked up his suit jacket and slipped it on as he headed for the hallway leading to the downstairs entrance. "I love you."

"Love you too!" CJ called after him. She moved to the window, standing there for several minutes until she saw Matt's car pull out onto the street below. With the beautiful weather, she looked forward to attending Matt's game after her evening practice.

On days like these, with Matt in town, CJ felt that her life was on track, at least in the most important area—her marriage. Still smiling, she turned away from the window and headed to the bedroom to get ready for swim practice.

* * *

The pool was quiet when CJ walked in for the first time after the trial. The lifeguard was still setting out gear in anticipation of the five o'clock practice that would begin in another ten minutes. CJ's coach wasn't on deck yet, and she reminded herself of the reason she had given him for missing practice. Not for the first time, the excuse was a family funeral; personally, CJ felt that excuse had been used far too often.

She dropped her bag onto a deck chair, noticing for the first time that the events for the upcoming meet had been posted on the team bulletin board. Nerves jumped in her stomach as she walked the few yards to the bulletin board. When she had signed up for the meet, she had planned to enter the 100-meter breaststroke, 200-meter breaststroke, and 200-meter individual medley.

Scanning the lineup, CJ finally found her name. Under it was listed only one event, the 200-meter breaststroke. She read over the list again, hoping there had been some mistake, but again she found that she was only listed as competing in the one event.

CJ began reading the events a third time, this time looking at the events her teammates were signed up for. Each of them had at least two events, some as many as five or six events. When she noticed Bridget Bannon's name, she read her events and shook her head. Bridget had been entered in both the 100- and 200-meter breaststroke events, both individual medleys, the 100-meter freestyle, and every relay.

As hard as she tried, CJ couldn't understand her coach's logic. Surely he would want her to swim in the 100-meter breaststroke and the 200-meter individual medley. She had posted the best times on the team during the past month, surpassing Bridget Bannon's times in both events. Why would he only enter her in the one event where Bridget would definitely beat her, and why would he give Bridget all of the relay spots when CJ was faster on the shorter breaststroke distances?

So sure that she could finally achieve her Olympic trials qualifying times in her best events, CJ shook her head in frustration. Then she saw her coach, Aaron, enter the pool area.

"So you made it back," he stated simply as he started to pass by her.

"I wanted to ask you about my event for this weekend."

Aaron sighed. "What about it?"

"I just wanted to know why I wasn't entered into any other events," CJ said.

"You missed practice," Aaron declared.

"What?" CJ stared at him with disbelief. "I was at a funeral. I was only gone thirty-six hours."

Aaron shrugged. "Look, you'll have a chance to swim in more events at the next meet. It's only a couple of weeks away."

"Will I be able to swim the 100 breast and the 200 IM?"

"We'll see." Aaron stepped away from her, glancing briefly over his shoulder. "We're already pretty set in those events."

At that moment, Bridget walked in from the locker room. CJ wondered if her heart had simply stopped when she realized for the first time what was happening. Bridget didn't want CJ anywhere near an event that CJ might win.

Anger flowing through her veins, CJ nearly turned and walked out of the building. But a more rational thought came quietly and clearly. *Where could I go?* Her body shook with anger as she dove in and began her workout. Despite her emotions, she found comfort as she glided through the water, swimming freestyle for her warm-up. As she put the yards behind her, anger gave way to logic, and she realized she could still get her qualifying time in the 200-meter breast-stroke the following weekend. It was a long shot for her to make the Olympics in the event, but at least she could qualify for the Olympic trials. But then what?

CJ didn't know how she could possibly change teams, and she knew that competing without a coach would be virtually impossible. She continued her workout, barely hearing anything her coach said. When Aaron finally lined the swimmers up for sprints, CJ noticed that Bridget waited for CJ to line up and chose to swim in a different group.

Her suspicions that Bridget didn't want to compete against her grew, and for the first time CJ glimpsed the depth of the politics that sometimes ruled the sports world.

* * *

Matt opened his door and forced his exhausted body to move up the stairs and into the bedroom he shared with CJ. He had fully planned on falling face-first into bed and letting himself slide into oblivion. That was until he saw the bed was empty.

He glanced at his watch, seeing that it was already after one o'clock in the morning. Surprised that CJ wasn't in bed, he moved down the hall to the living room. She was curled up on the couch, her eyes swollen and her cheeks tearstained. The only light in the room came from the flames flickering in the fireplace in front of her.

"What's wrong?"

CJ just shook her head. Tears threatened, but she swallowed hard. "My coach isn't going to let me swim the 100. I can't qualify if I can't swim it."

Matt looked at her more closely, surprised to see defeat in her eyes. He couldn't ever remember a time when she had given up on anything. "Why won't he let you swim it?"

"I think it's because I can beat Bridget." CJ swiped at a stray tear as he sat down next to her.

"What makes you say that?" Matt reached his arm around her shoulders, pulling her close.

"It's the only thing that makes sense. Bridget's family practically owns this team, and no one wants to upset the balance, least of all the coach." CJ leaned her head against his shoulder. "I beat her twice in practice last week, both times in the 100 breaststroke, yet Aaron gave Bridget the spot in the medley relay. The only event he signed me up for is the 200 breast, which is the one thing Bridget can beat me in. When I asked Aaron if I could swim the 100 breast and the 200 IM in the next meet, he said that they were pretty set in those races."

"CJ, you're going to have to switch teams."

CJ shifted so that she could see him more clearly. "Matt, do you understand what that would mean? The Olympic trials are three months away. No coach in his right mind would pick up a new swimmer this late in the game."

"Then do it without a coach," Matt suggested.

"I don't think I can."

"Look, why don't you see how this meet goes?" Matt asked. "Doug is nervous enough about you competing. It might be a good thing that you're only swimming one of your weaker events. If the focus stays on Bridget, hopefully the wrong people won't notice you."

"I guess."

"Come on." Matt stood up and, with little effort, scooped CJ off of the couch. "It's time for bed."

CJ reached up and kissed her husband. "I'm glad you're home."

"Me too."

* * *

CJ's team was spread out in a corner of the pool area, some playing cards, others watching the meet, and still others preparing to swim. CJ stood apart, needing the space both physically and emotionally from the coach she had thought would support her Olympic dreams.

Deep down, the seed had been planted. Did he think she wasn't good enough to compete in the Olympics, or did he really just want to protect the swimmer he had been training for nearly a decade? Bridget had been competing consistently since her childhood. CJ hadn't been in a single meet in almost a year.

She pushed the negative thoughts aside, trying instead to think about Matt's baseball game. She held a miniature radio in her hand, one earpiece in her right ear so she could listen to the game and the other earpiece hanging free so she could hear the swim-meet events being announced. Matt had not come into the game yet, and she was hopeful that he would get at least a few innings. After all, if he was going to spend the next three days in New York, he should at least get the chance to play.

Out of the corner of her eye, CJ glimpsed Aaron giving Bridget some last minute instructions before she began her warm-up for the 200-meter breaststroke. CJ stayed where she was, already aware that she wouldn't receive the same level of attention. For the past two days at practice, Aaron had hardly spoken to her except when he instructed the team as a group.

Bridget had decided the day before to skip practice so that she could rest, yet no changes had been made to her events despite missing nearly as much pool time as CJ had earlier in the week.

The commentator on the radio announced a pitching change as CJ pulled her earpiece out and tucked her radio inside her bag. Nerves fluttered in her stomach, a sense of anticipation to finally race again. She grabbed her towel and pulled off her shorts and T-shirt before heading to the warm-up lanes. Bridget was already in the pool, smoothly cutting through the water.

CJ chose a different lane and began swimming freestyle to loosen up. A few minutes later, she switched to breast-stroke, working on a few turns and her stroke count before getting out of the pool to check in for her race.

She tried not to think about the fact that Bridget was in the lane next to her. The coach's time CJ had been entered with was from a timed swim a few weeks before. Although she knew her times had been dropping over the past few weeks, she hadn't expected to be seeded as one of the top swimmers with just a practice time. For swimmers' entry times, coaches normally used times clocked in previous meets, since that was where swimmers typically had their fastest times. Practice times tended to be inherently slower than race results because it was hard to re-create the compet-itive atmosphere and adrenaline rush of an actual meet.

When CJ reached her lane, she let herself visualize the race. She swam it so often in practice, yet so many months had passed since she last felt that rush of adrenaline that came only from competition. Could she make the cut for the Olympic trials, and if so, could she possibly make it to the Olympics in this event?

As the defending world champion, Bridget was expected to take first place at the Olympic trials and the pressure was already on her to bring home the gold. *They take two from each event,* CJ reminded herself. The first- and second-place finishers in each event at the Olympic trials would make the Olympic team. Even if Bridget's times were out of her reach, CJ could still try to claim the second-place spot at the trials.

The swimmer on the other side of her leaned down over the side of the pool and splashed water on herself. Having dried off after her warm-up, CJ opted to stay dry until she started her race. She didn't mind the shock of the cold water. In fact, she was convinced that the rush of cold water helped her shake off the lingering nerves that she always struggled with while waiting for her race to start.

Staring out over the pool in front of her, CJ pressed her goggles into place as her heat was announced. When the whistle blew, she stepped up onto the block, her heart racing. A hush came over the crowd for the beginning of the race as the starter's voice sounded through the starting system and commanded them to take their marks.

The buzzer sounded and CJ dove into the water with her competition. The shock of the cold water lasted only a second, and CJ let her body take over. She held her body in a tight, streamlined position until she felt the momentum from her dive start to slow. Then she pulled both arms down past her waist, increasing the speed at which her body flew through the water. The moment she felt her speed decreasing, her powerful kick thrust her forward, and she surfaced to begin her first full stroke.

She pushed her arms up and out over the water's surface, squeezing her shoulders forward to reduce the resistance her body would create as she moved through the water. She found her rhythm early and reminded herself not to focus on the swimmers next to her but rather to concentrate on the race she planned to swim. She tried to increase her speed as she approached the first turn, nervousness still humming through her.

When she hit the 50-meter mark, CJ saw that she had already negated the lead Bridget had taken at the start. At the halfway point, they were still dead even. Not until the last turn did Bridget's height advantage manifest itself. CJ saw Bridget pulling away, and she concentrated on letting her kick push her efficiently through the water as she attempted to stay close to Bridget. Despite CJ's efforts, she still finished nearly two seconds behind Bridget.

CJ looked up at the scoreboard, a grin crossing her face when she saw that her time had qualified her for the Olympic trials. She rested on the lane line between her lane and Bridget's, stretching out her hand. "Nice swim, Bridget."

Bridget glanced at CJ's hand before turning her back on CJ and climbing out of the pool.

CJ looked after her, surprised at the complete lack of sportsmanship.

"Don't worry about her," a voice came from behind her.

CJ turned to see the girl that had placed a few seconds behind her leaning with both arms over the lane rope. "You had a great swim. She isn't used to having someone push her that hard."

"Thanks." CJ accepted the girl's outstretched hand and then pulled herself out of the pool. She turned back and added, "Good luck with the rest of the meet."

"You too," the girl called after her, unaware that CJ was already finished.

CHAPTER 4

Doug Valdez crossed the street to his office building, a bottle of orange juice in one hand and a bagel in the other. Only a year ago he would have skipped breakfast, opting instead for a cup of coffee. Now he had to function at the break of dawn without the aid of caffeine. He still wasn't sure how this whole transformation had happened.

It was all Jill's fault. He never would have started reading the Book of Mormon had it not been for her. Well, perhaps CJ shared in the blame—or the credit, as the case may be. He had seen enough divine intervention in her life to wonder about the Latter-day Saints and their religion. In fact, he had been in the middle of one of CJ's miracles when he realized that he too had started relying on the Lord's help and guidance.

Doug took a sip of orange juice as he entered the elevator, thinking of the expressions on his parents' faces when he had told them he was getting baptized into the Church. To say that they were completely shocked was definitely an understatement. Still, they had attended his baptism, and just a few months ago his sister had commented on how much happier he seemed since meeting Jill.

Sighing in resignation, Doug decided he was going to have to thank CJ one of these days. If he hadn't been assigned to her, he wouldn't have met Jill or started investigating the Church. He could hardly believe that he was only a few months away from getting married in the temple—definitely not an aspiration he had ever expected to have. Now he couldn't think of anything he wanted more.

His transfer to Miami had come earlier than he would have liked, separating him and Jill for the last few months before their wedding. He just kept reminding himself that in a couple of months, it would all be worth it.

Phones rang and the scent of coffee lingered when Doug entered the FBI's Miami office. The far wall of the large office was lined with huge windows, and partitions divided the room up into cubicles to afford some privacy.

He sat down at his desk and glanced at his watch for the third time in less than ten minutes. In just three more hours, his fiancée would arrive from Texas to spend a week house hunting with him. The details for their wedding seemed to be endless, and Doug found that the only good thing about being transferred to Miami before their wedding was that it got him out of helping make all of those insignificant decisions. He didn't want to tell Jill that he thought the color of her bridesmaids' dresses was irrelevant. At this point all he wanted was to actually be married to her so that they could start their life together.

A schoolteacher, Jill planned to finish out the school year with her second-grade class, which prevented her from moving to Miami before the wedding, as Doug had hoped she would. She had also pointed out how difficult it would be to plan a wedding in Texas if she was living in Florida.

Before Doug could check his watch again, the phone rang. When he picked it up, the receptionist blurted out, "You have a visitor in the reception area," then hung up without telling him the person's name. Doug walked to the lobby, surprised to see Tara Baldino, one of the U.S. Marshals intermittently assigned to protect CJ over the last two years.

"Is there someplace we can talk privately?" Tara asked before Doug had a chance to greet her.

"Yeah, come on into the conference room." Doug led her down the hall and opened a heavy door.

Tara passed through the door and sat down in one of the chairs surrounding the mahogany table. She slid a file folder across the table as Doug took a seat.

"What's going on?"

"It looks like CJ is now our only witness."

"What?" Panic crept up Doug's spine as he flipped open the file. The top sheet outlined the death of Tom Miller—a.k.a. Leonard Abbott—in a scuba-diving accident.

"What was Abbott doing in Aruba?"

"Apparently he won some free trip down there. He went out scuba diving with a bunch of other tourists. The instructor said that Miller strayed off by himself, and when he tried to get him to rejoin the group, Miller panicked and surfaced too fast. By the time they got him to the hospital, he was already dead."

"Where was his protection?" Doug asked, flipping through the file.

"Abbott never told us he was going on a vacation, so we didn't know anything about it until we went in for a routine check of his cover."

"His wife didn't tell you what happened?"

"She didn't even think of it." Tara shook her head with disbelief. "When we went in for the cover check, she was already packing up and getting ready to move. She said she didn't have our number, and she didn't want to live in Boise anymore."

"You have got to be kidding me." Doug shook his head and pushed back from the table. He paced across the room, raking his fingers through his short, dark hair. "Leonard Abbott, the guy who's afraid of his own shadow, picks up and goes on vacation without a word to anyone?"

"Apparently so." Tara leaned back in her chair while Doug absorbed the new information. "His wife said that they used to go on vacations every year so that he could go scuba diving and she could spend time with the kids at the beach. I guess he figured he'd had enough of Boise for the winter and decided to take the free vacation when it came his way."

"Doesn't that sound a little odd, that he would just happen to win a trip for the kind of vacation he always used to take?" Doug asked. "And that an experienced diver would surface too fast?" Doug hesitated for a moment and then asked, "Did he still have air in his tank?"

"The air level on the tank was about the same as everyone else's who had gone on the dive with him. They all started with full tanks, and they all had over an hour's worth of air left." Tara pushed back from the table and stood. "Look, Doug. There's no evidence of foul play, but that doesn't mean there wasn't any. I think we have to assume that somehow Rush's men found Abbott. For all we know, CJ is next."

"Not if I can help it."

"Not if *we* can help it," Tara amended.

"How soon can you be in Philadelphia?" Doug asked.

"I fly out in an hour." Tara reached into her purse and pulled out a thick envelope. "I've got something for you. Consider it an early wedding present."

Doug opened the envelope and pulled out two tickets to Aruba, one for him and one for Jill.

Tara walked to the door and glanced over her shoulder at Doug. "I thought we might feel better if someone took a closer look. I didn't think your fiancée would mind a few days on the beach."

A smile crossed Doug's face. "I think I can talk her into it."

* * *

Doug stood by a window in the airport, relieved to see that Jill's plane had finally made it to the gate. The flight was only ten minutes late, but the window of time they had to retrieve Jill's luggage and then check in for their flight to Aruba was already tight. Anticipating that Jill wouldn't have time to eat before their next flight—the flight she didn't know about yet— Doug held a pizza in one hand and a water bottle in the other.

The waiting area near the gate was empty except for the airline employee waiting to assist the passengers. Doug had used his FBI credentials to pass through security, and he now moved closer to where Jill would exit the plane.

The door finally opened. The first people off the plane were the first-class passengers—businessmen walking with obvious destinations in mind and schedules to keep. A mix of families and tourists came next, blending in with those that were harder to categorize.

Doug watched more than a hundred passengers deplane before he finally caught a glimpse of Jill. She was tall and slender, and her cap of blond hair was cropped short, a fringe of bangs falling over a face that many thought should grace the covers of magazines. The woman in front of her had a baby in her arms. Doug wasn't surprised to see Jill holding hands with the woman's other two children, a little boy of about five and a curly-haired girl who carried a stuffed dog that was nearly as big as she was.

Not expecting to see him at the gate, Jill didn't even look up, instead talking to the little girl as they walked into the waiting area. Her eyes widened when Doug moved forward into her view.

"I see you're making new friends again." Doug grinned, moving forward to kiss her on the cheek.

"Tyler and Emily were keeping me company," Jill explained before turning them back over to their mother. The woman thanked Jill for her help before being swept away by the crowd. Jill turned back toward Doug, spotting the pizza he held.

"Is that for me?" Jill asked, falling into step with Doug as they moved toward the baggage claim.

"I thought you might be hungry, and it will be a while until we get a chance to eat again." Doug handed her the pizza and took her by the arm, guiding her through the crowd.

Jill trotted along, barely able to keep up with his pace. "Are we in a hurry?"

"Actually, yes," Doug said as he sidestepped a woman pushing a stroller. "I'm afraid we have a pretty tight schedule today." Before she could answer, he added, "Do you have your passport with you?"

Jill's eyebrows shot up. "Yeah, I was going to ask you about that. Someone from your office called and told me to bring my passport with me. Why do I need a passport in Miami?"

"Actually, she wasn't from my office. She was just helping me out with something."

They stepped onto the escalator that led down to the baggage claim area. "Doug, what's going on?"

"I have a little business I need to take care of, and I thought you wouldn't mind tagging along."

"As long as you promise I won't get shot at."

"If I thought that was a possibility, I wouldn't invite you," Doug said wryly.

Jill shrugged her shoulders and tried to look serious, but her voice was full of fun when she spoke. "I'm just making sure. After you made me learn to shoot your gun, I thought maybe you were trying to recruit me."

"Very funny." Doug shook his head, fighting back a grin. "Actually, we're going on a little trip. We should have just enough time to transfer your luggage over before we board."

"What?" Jill stepped off at the bottom of the escalator, moving out of the way of other travelers and stopping. She motioned for Doug to do the same.

Anticipating her next question, Doug handed her the tickets. He watched her expression change as she read their destination. "I need to do a little poking around down there for a day or two, but we should still have plenty of time to hang out on the beach, maybe go snorkeling."

"Are you serious?" Jill's eyes lit up. "You're taking me to Aruba for the weekend?"

"You don't mind, do you?" Doug asked playfully.

Jill's laughter rang out. "Let's just hurry up and get my bags."

* * *

Nearly a week had passed since CJ's swim meet, and the tension at practice continued to grow. Several of their teammates had noticed Bridget's response to CJ at the meet the weekend before, and rumors buzzed in the locker room for days about the friction between the two of them. Unfortunately, the odd behavior from her coach also continued.

Similar to his behavior during the few days before the meet, Aaron made few specific suggestions about CJ's strokes, almost as if he were afraid to be seen talking to her. The two times CJ had tried to talk to him about the meet scheduled for the following week, he had made quick excuses and left her wondering what she should do. She had not even been able to verify if the coach was going to enter her in the meet.

As Friday afternoon practice came to an end, CJ climbed out of the pool and grabbed her towel. She dried off her face, looked up, and froze. Tara Baldino, U.S. Marshal, stood in front of her. CJ forced herself to take a deep breath. *Why is Tara here? Has something happened? Is something bad going to happen?* A myriad of thoughts raced through CJ's mind in what seemed like only a split second.

Stepping forward, Tara put a hand on her shoulder. "I was in the neighborhood. I thought we could go grab a bite to eat together, maybe go catch the Phillies game."

"Sure." CJ tried to sound casual. "Do I have time to shower and change?"

Tara nodded, an unspoken message passing between them. "Take your time."

When CJ walked out of the building a few minutes later, Tara motioned to a car parked nearby. "Let's take my car. We can pick yours up on the way home."

Still curious, CJ slid into the passenger's seat, anxiously awaiting the privacy the car would give them. As soon as Tara started up the engine, she turned to CJ.

"We don't think anything is wrong—I'm just here to make sure."

"What happened?" CJ asked. When Tara turned to look at her, CJ added, "I've been under for too long not to know that U.S. Marshals don't just show up on your doorstep without a reason."

Tara took a deep breath. "Leonard Abbott is dead."

"What?" CJ asked, her eyes widening. "How?"

"It looks like a scuba diving accident."

"Looks like . . ." CJ keyed in on her words. "You aren't convinced."

"Doug is headed down to Aruba to look into it more closely." Tara shrugged. "For all we know, it was an accident. But regardless of how it happened, the result is the same. You are back to being our only witness against Rush."

"Wonderful," CJ sighed. "So you're here just in case it wasn't an accident."

"Basically," Tara agreed. "We'll give Doug a couple of days to poke around and see if there's anything suspicious before we decide what to do next."

"I thought Jill was visiting him this week to go house hunting," CJ commented, thinking that her former roommate was not going to be pleased if she flew to Miami only to have her fiancé fly out.

"She's going along with him." Tara winked at her. "I thought it was the least I could do since her plans were interrupted."

"A trip to the sun and sand," CJ laughed. "I think she'll forgive the interruption."

Tara motioned to a strip of restaurants. "Did you want to go grab something to eat?"

"You do realize that the Phillies are on a road trip."

Tara nodded.

"In that case, how about heading back to my place and ordering some pizza?" CJ suggested. "I'm sure you're going to want to check out my building anyway."

"We already have," Tara laughed. "If you don't mind, I'm going to stay with you until Matt gets back, and Mark Lacey will be in a hotel down the street."

"Where is Lacey?" CJ asked.

"He's checking out your car, just to be on the safe side. As soon as it's clear, he'll drive it back here for you," Tara informed her. "Now for the more important issue, what kind of pizza are we ordering?"

CJ laughed as she and Tara debated for several minutes whether or not onions actually belonged on pizza and about the health issues surrounding processed meats. Forty-five minutes later, they were both stretched out in front of the television watching the Phillies game, CJ working her way through a second piece of extra-boring cheese pizza, and Tara munching on a slice of meat lover's.

"Are you all set for the meet next weekend?" Tara asked after finishing off three slices.

"I don't know. My coach won't talk to me about it, and the way he was talking last week, I don't think he's even going to put me in my two main events," CJ said. She proceeded to explain the events of the past two weeks, including the problems she suspected came from the competition she was now giving Bridget.

"These opportunities don't come around often enough for you to sit them out," Tara replied. "I think we may have to just pull a few strings and get you into the right events."

"If I show up for the meet and my coach sees me swimming in the 100 breaststroke and the 200 IM, he'll just go in and scratch me from them."

"Then you have to quit this team before next weekend."

"Tara, do you have any idea what that means? I'm not going to be able to find another coach only three months before the Olympic trials."

Tara turned and looked her in the eye. "What are the chances that this coach is going to help you get to the Olympics?"

CJ sighed. "About one in a million."

"Then you don't have anything to lose."

* * *

The pool on the Penn State campus was nearly empty when CJ walked inside the building. She didn't know how the marshals had obtained a school ID for her so quickly, but she had stopped asking those kinds of questions months ago. Tara followed her into the pool area and pointed to a nearby chair. "I'll be right here if you need me."

CJ nodded, dropping her swim bag by the side of the pool. After donning her cap and goggles, she dove into the pool and began her warm-up. She had drafted her own workouts for the next week, but she was still praying that Doug or Tara would be able to find her a new coach.

Basic workouts she could do; tapering workouts she couldn't. The practice of tapering was widely used in swimming, pounding out difficult yards and pushing an athlete to the brink of exhaustion, then resting that athlete to bring out peak performance. How could CJ possibly determine her own limits? Tapering was something only done once or twice a year and was definitely not something that she knew how to do on her own.

Quitting her team had been less painful than she expected. Although CJ had imagined a confrontation with Aaron, Tara had eliminated that possibility by writing him a letter. In a straightforward and tactful manner, Tara explained that CJ planned to take more control of her competitive swimming career. CJ had signed the letter with a sigh of relief.

After completing a long warm-up, CJ pulled a kickboard and fins out of her bag. She slipped the short fins on her feet and started across the pool with the kickboard in front of her. She noticed a lap swimmer a few lanes over and wondered how crowded the pool would be during her afternoon practice.

She pushed through her planned practice, occasionally stopping to check her notes. When she came to the end of her practice, she looked up at the clock, surprised to see that she still had forty-five minutes left. Annoyed that she had miscalculated her workout, especially after spending so much time planning it, CJ set out to swim another set that she hoped would use up the rest of her time.

Though she tried to keep her thoughts positive, CJ realized that a coach might be more of a necessity than anyone realized.

CHAPTER 5

Leaning on the railing of her hotel-room balcony, Jill looked over the water just a short distance away. The waves rolled lazily over the sand, the roar of the ocean filling the air.

Despite the palm trees surrounding the hotels along the main strip in Palm Beach, Aruba was not the lush tropical island Jill had imagined. A dry desert breeze ruffled her short hair as she bit into the pastry she had ordered from room service. A few ambitious souls jogged along the beach despite the early hour.

Jill glanced at her watch, wondering how much longer she should wait before calling Doug's room to see if he was up. They had arrived so late the night before that they had barely managed to find a restaurant still open to serve them dinner. Doug had been his usual closemouthed self until they had finally gotten to their hotel.

He hadn't told her much, but Jill knew enough about this particular case to understand the result of Leonard Abbott's death. Throughout the night her mind had been filled with concern for her former roommate, now known as CJ.

Everything had seemed so normal when she and CJ had lived together in Texas. Though CJ's real name was Christal Jones, at the time she had been using the alias Kylie Ramsey. Despite the fact that she was in the Witness Protection

Program, she had made a full life for herself. She spent her time swimming, going to school, and dating Matt Whitmore—an up-and-coming baseball player. Jill had met and started dating Doug.

Then in a single instant everything had changed. Jill remembered all too well the day CJ disappeared from Texas, the day Doug had barely managed to sneak her past the men sent to kill her. Even now, Jill could only pray that Doug and those working with him would be astute enough to see danger coming before it was too late.

Walking back into her room, Jill glanced at her watch again. She waited until almost eight before she dialed the number for Doug's room. The phone rang five times before she finally hung up. *Maybe he's in the shower,* she thought to herself, wondering when he would be ready to go out and see the island.

Less than a minute later, a knock sounded at her door. She opened it up to find Doug standing in the hall. "Good, you're already up." Doug leaned in and gave her a quick kiss. "Are you ready to head out?"

Jill nodded. "I've been ready."

"I should have known you would be anxious to get the day started. I went out and rented a car. It's parked out front."

They made their way to the elevators and then outside to the tiny hatchback. He shrugged and opened the passenger door for her. "Beggars can't be choosers."

"As long as it gets us where we're going," Jill said. As soon as he pulled out of the parking lot, she added, "So where are we going?"

"I thought you might be willing to do a little poking around with me."

"What kind of poking?" Jill asked suspiciously.

"I wanted to start at the dive shop that Abbott used the day he died."

"You don't expect me to go scuba diving with them, do you?"

"No, actually, I want you to go in and pretend you're thinking about it. You know, ask a bunch of questions," Doug explained. He went on to point out the specific information he needed based on what he had gleaned from the initial reports and suggested how she might lead the conversation where he wanted it to go.

When they arrived at the dive shop, Jill approached the place alone. A boat was already preparing to set out, and Jill thought she might have already missed her opportunity to talk to the dive instructors. She passed by the modest dive shop and walked toward the dock, noticing several air tanks that were waiting to be loaded on the boat. A man in his late twenties stepped off the boat and headed toward her.

"Hi there," Jill greeted him, moving aside as he approached the air tanks.

The man smiled, glimpsing the strap of her swimsuit beneath her T-shirt. "Are you here for a dive?"

"No, actually, I've never gone scuba diving before."

"Well, we can set you up if you're interested," he told her with a grin. "You will have to take one of our certification courses, but it only takes a morning, and then you can be diving with an instructor as soon as this afternoon."

"I'm still not sure I'm ready to breathe my air out of one of those." Jill pointed to the air tanks.

"It takes a little getting used to, but it's really easy."

"How does it work? I mean, how can you tell how much air you have and how long you can stay under?"

"Let me show you," he motioned for her to follow him into a room full of dive equipment. He showed her the basic equipment, explaining how the air gauges worked and how each diver rented the necessary equipment and weights if they didn't have their own.

"Those air tanks over there," Jill started as she stepped back outside, "are they for specific people, or do you just give them to whoever needs one?"

"Usually if people need an air tank, they sign up the night before so that we have them ready by morning."

Jill saw Doug come out of the dive shop and head toward her. Doug nodded at the man and put a proprietary hand on Jill's shoulder. "Has he convinced you that it's safe yet?"

"I just don't know if I want to try that." Jill forced herself to shudder. "I mean with what happened to that poor man a couple of weeks ago." Jill turned back toward the dive instructor. "I'm sure you heard about it, the diving accident?"

The man tensed briefly before responding. "That was unfortunate, but if the guy had stayed with his instructor, it never would have happened."

"He went off on his own?" Jill asked incredulously.

The instructor nodded. "Apparently he lost touch with the rest of his group and panicked. I guess he tried to surface too fast because by the time the instructor found him, he was already dead."

Jill turned back to look at Doug. "If it's all the same to you, I think I'll stick with snorkeling."

"I had a feeling you would say that." Doug nodded to the instructor. "Have a good one."

Jill waited until Doug pulled out into the light traffic before asking, "What did you find out?"

"Not much. Everything seems to agree with the witness reports that Abbott went on the advanced dive and apparently went off on his own."

"It *could* have happened that way." Jill shrugged.

"His wife said that he's been scuba diving for years. It just doesn't add up that an experienced diver would surface too fast."

"Maybe something was wrong with his equipment."

"The island police said they checked it out and it was fine."

"Then Abbott was either out of practice and got careless, or someone did a great job of making it look like an accident."

"I just wish I could find something that would tell me which one." Doug pulled the car into a parking lot near the marina.

"What are we doing here?"

"I thought we could go for a sail."

"I think I can handle that." Jill grinned.

* * *

The woman who owned the sailboat Doug had chartered lived below deck when she wasn't working. Shirley had left her home in Miami nearly fifteen years before, and she chattered on about the history of the island, the tourism industry, and the constant influx of tourists from the U.S. Her skin was weathered from the sun and the wind, making her look about fifty years old, but Doug guessed that she was closer to forty.

Doug only had to ask a couple of general questions about scuba diving before Shirley started rambling on about the accident. The news was still fresh on the island, and she was already worried about how the bad press might affect tourism and the diving industry in the future.

Above them the sails billowed in the wind, and except for an occasional boat, most of the water traffic was far behind them. Doug studied the island, anticipating from the curve of the land that they were nearing the site where Abbott had died.

Jill moved onto the deck to soak up some sun. Her simple blue swimsuit was a modest one-piece, and she had carefully applied sunscreen to protect herself against the hot sun. Doug wished that he could have relaxed on deck with her and just enjoyed the view.

Turning away from his beautiful fiancée, Doug sat with his back to her and tried to glean from Shirley's wealth of knowledge of local diving spots. Still listening to her, Doug absorbed her descriptions of the dive sites as they approached Malmok Reef. From the map he had studied earlier, it was one of only four dive sites along this section of the island.

When Shirley stopped to take a breath, Doug asked, "Do a lot of people come out and use these sites?"

"It varies. Most people go to the sites that are closer to the hotels. These take a bit longer to get to." Shirley pointed farther out to sea. "That one over there is a beginner dive, so it's used pretty frequently. Apparently some beginners were diving over there around the time the accident occurred here at Malmok."

"Was the other group still around when the accident happened?"

Shirley shook her head. "I heard they were already long gone. The beginner group usually only goes down for forty-five minutes or so. That site is only about thirty-five feet deep."

"What about this one?" Doug asked as she slowed near Malmok Reef.

"It's about twice that. Seventy feet, give or take a few."

"Sounds kind of deep," Doug commented.

"Not really. Even beginners sometimes go down forty or fifty feet." Shirley shrugged. "Seventy isn't that bad for someone who has some experience."

"Sounds like he wasn't experienced enough." Doug turned and studied Malmok Reef. The beginner dive site was some distance away, far enough that the beginners probably would not have noticed anything suspicious. *It was perfect,*

Doug thought. Just deep enough for Abbott to get into trouble, but not quite deep enough to raise suspicions.

Doug glanced up at Jill. *She's right,* he thought to himself. Either Abbott really had gotten careless, or someone had gone to great lengths to make his death look like an accident.

CHAPTER 6

Jimmy Malloy stepped out of the rental car and looked up at the federal building. It was a gamble to come himself, but Malloy liked to think of it as a calculated risk. He supposed he should be uncomfortable visiting a jail, fully aware that dozens of his past actions could land him inside these walls as a resident rather than as a visitor. Malloy didn't like to entertain such thoughts, however, so he pushed them aside and concentrated on the situation at hand.

In another month, Chris Rush would either become a permanent resident of the federal penitentiary or of the local morgue. Malloy had done enough poking around to know that the girl testifying against him was well hidden. If he couldn't find her through traditional channels, he doubted anyone else would either. Of course, he didn't particularly care for traditional channels. The reward for Christal Jones's death was a hefty one, and collecting it was just one of the possible outcomes of Malloy's current plans.

For now, however, he had more pressing matters to attend to. The legal expenses Rush was piling up had been causing a cash drain on the organization for some time. Now that the trial was just around the corner, Rush was once again depleting his operational funds to attain the location of the girl.

Rebuilding was expensive, and Malloy needed another influx of cash so that he could maintain the standard of living he had grown accustomed to. He couldn't cut Rush off from his funds without risking some kind of reprisal from those still loyal to Rush within the organization. Instead, he had turned his attention to other possible sources. Taking care of the girl would give him a nice little windfall of money, and then there were the diamonds.

A stash of diamonds had been lost three years before when a cop had infiltrated deep into their operations. Malloy knew that the cop had taken the diamonds, presumably for evidence. Unfortunately, Malloy's men had killed the cop before the stones were recovered.

Some subtle probing had convinced Malloy that the diamonds were still out there somewhere. Originally, he hadn't concerned himself with the missing gems, but most of the current profits were needed to cover the high operational costs necessary to rebuild his empire. Malloy figured twenty million dollars worth of precious stones would give him just enough to tide him over until Rush was removed from the company one way or another.

His research had revealed that the two men convicted of killing the cop wouldn't have had time to stash the diamonds before they were arrested, and Malloy's search into those close to the two convicts revealed nothing remotely suspicious.

Malloy's investigation of the cop's family had convinced him that they hadn't discovered the diamonds either. The search of the cop's apartment had been more thorough than he had first believed, and none of the people involved in the case had suddenly come into any money. That left the girl.

Rush knew more about her than did anyone else within the organization. He also had the most reasons to want her dead—reasons that contributed to Malloy's unlikely visit to the federal jail.

Malloy handed over his fake ID and plucked a piece of lint off the sleeve of his Armani jacket. The security officer took his name and told him to take a seat. Malloy stood. He was not about to sit on one of the filthy chairs in the waiting room.

Ten minutes later his name was called, and he was led into the visiting area. He retrieved a handkerchief from his inside pocket and wiped off the vinyl seat before sitting down. While he waited for Rush to be brought in, he picked up the telephone receiver and wiped that down as well.

The man that sat down opposite him was not the formidable man Malloy remembered. His normally tanned skin was chalky white, and he had deep circles under his eyes. Those dark eyes had once been capable of dropping a man with a single glance, had once emanated power, authority, control. Now they just looked evil. The once-athletic build now appeared thin, almost fragile in the bright orange prison uniform.

Rush picked up the receiver on his side of the security glass. "What are you doing here?"

"Just thought I would pay a visit to an old friend," Malloy stated calmly.

"If you had honored our agreement, I wouldn't be here for you to visit," Rush hissed over the phone.

"I'm working on that." Malloy aimed a meaningful look at the guard in the corner of the room. "I also wanted to ask you about the merchandise you lost several years ago."

Rush's eyes sparked with interest, and he leaned back in his seat, a remnant of his former self returning.

Malloy continued, "Did you know the courier's girlfriend well?"

Rush's lips snarled somewhere between a grin and a grimace. "I only met her once. Pretty girl. Dark hair, smoky eyes. A very talented swimmer. Breaststroke was her favorite, I believe."

Malloy leaned back as he spoke companionably with Rush. "Tell me, did she have any good luck charms she liked to keep with her? Something your courier might have given her?"

Rush shook his head and sneered. "The diamonds are gone. Don't waste your time."

"It happens I have bit of free time on my hands." Malloy stood, brushing absently at his slacks. Without a backwards glance, he strode out of the room.

* * *

"I don't like it," Doug spoke into his cell phone as he paced his office. After spending three days in Aruba, he and Jill had returned the day before, and he had been working ever since. Thankfully, Jill had offered to go out with the realtor by herself to start narrowing down their housing choices.

Keith Toblin's voice came through the line. "I can't say I'm crazy about the idea either, but the marshals have a valid argument. We know that the hotel reservations have been traced through our travel system. They think she will be safer if the FBI isn't involved."

"You know as well as I do that she isn't the typical Witness Protection Program candidate. The FBI has been running the show since she went underground."

"I had this same argument with the marshals. They insisted that the only way they will approve the security plan is if they have complete control." Keith's sigh came over the line. "We both know how much this meet means to CJ, and two marshals are going to be with her at all times."

"I still don't like it," Doug stated firmly.

"Neither do I."

* * *

CJ sat in the waiting area of the Philadelphia airport, her earphones on so that she could hear the ball game on her palm-sized radio. The afternoon game had been delayed by nearly an hour because of a passing thunderstorm that had come through just as the game was scheduled to start. CJ had hoped to hear the whole game before her four o'clock flight, but now she was just hoping the clouds in the distance wouldn't cause any more trouble.

Keith Toblin sat beside her, the latest edition of *Sports Illustrated* in his hand. CJ knew the magazine was just a prop, despite the two marshals who were hovering nearby. One of the marshals would be on the same flight as CJ, routing through Chicago before heading to Minneapolis. Tara would take a direct flight into Minneapolis, arriving early enough to secure their transportation and hotel accommodations.

CJ noticed the other passengers preparing to board, but she waited until the line was nearly gone before she stood and picked up her duffel bag.

"I'll see you in a couple of days," Keith said as she headed for the gate.

CJ nodded, knowing that he would remain close by until she was safely in the air. The marshal that was traveling with her had already boarded, and CJ was not surprised to see him settled in a seat two rows behind her.

He looked like a typical business traveler, wearing a suit and tapping away on his laptop. CJ tried to think of the marshal that way in an effort to control the nerves that always surfaced when she traveled. Even with Doug's assurances that the latest leak had been plugged, she always wondered when Rush would manage to create a new one.

The flight was uneventful, as was the second leg of their journey. Tara was waiting for CJ when she passed by the security area in Minneapolis. Darkness was already falling when they arrived at their hotel, and CJ was happy to use room service for a quiet meal alone.

After eating her dinner, CJ repacked her duffel bag for the next day. She checked and re-checked her goggles, made sure she had two spare caps, and then made sure her race suit and identification were in order.

By nine o'clock, CJ climbed into bed and turned the television to ESPN news. The highlights for the Phillies' game were brief, and she was disappointed to see that Matt's team had lost. She didn't even catch a glimpse of him on TV.

Restless, she turned off the television and tried to sink into unconsciousness. The hotel room was quiet, but her mind refused to shut down. She thought of the meet the next day, the expected confrontations with her former coach and teammates, even the potential danger she might face.

She hungered to hear Matt's voice, to listen to his version of the game that night and gain comfort from the encouragement he would give her. Unfortunately, Matt's schedule was such that the only way she could contact him was on his cell phone, and she knew her security team would never allow that. She still didn't quite understand how cell phone calls could be intercepted, but Doug had explained that intelligence believed that Rush's organization had the special equipment necessary to pick up cell phone calls, and that they were very adept at using it.

Finally, around midnight, CJ dropped off into a deep sleep.

* * *

"Hey, wake up." Doug nudged his fiancée as he noticed her closed eyes.

Jill shifted on the couch next to him and looked up at him in a daze. "I'm sorry. What time is it?"

"Almost midnight." Doug brushed at the short blond hair falling across her forehead. She was simply beautiful in every way, and he was already counting down the days until they would be sealed in the Dallas temple. Besides the fact that she would finally be living in Miami with him instead of a thousand miles away, he wanted more moments like these when he could just be with her.

Jill studied his face for a moment, all hard planes and angles shadowed with a day's worth of beard. Her eyes narrowed as she became fully awake. "Something's going on with CJ this weekend, isn't it?"

"Why would you think that?" Doug asked evasively. He already worried about how easily Jill could read his moods and analyze what triggered them.

"Doug, you've been working like a demon since we got back to Miami, and then suddenly you just want to hang out and watch TV. You even offered to spend the whole weekend going over wedding plans, something you hate to do, and you've checked your cell phone messages about a dozen times tonight." Jill's eyes met his. "That tells me something is going on at work, and after our trip to Aruba, I'm guessing it has to do with CJ."

"Have you ever considered a career in law enforcement?"

"I have a career in law enforcement." Jill laughed, thinking of her sometimes-unruly second-grade class. "I just try to *prevent* crime."

Doug grinned, knowing her statement wasn't far from the truth. He stood up, pulling her up with him. "I'll take you back to your hotel and let you get some sleep."

"Okay," Jill agreed, picking up her purse before heading outside. Half an hour later, Doug escorted her up to her room and waited while she unlocked the door.

Jill reached up and touched her lips briefly to his before stepping inside her room. She laughed when he pulled her closer to kiss her again. With one last kiss, he released her.

Doug took a step down the hall before turning back to Jill once more. "Remember to say your prayers tonight."

Jill nodded, knowing that he was indeed worried about CJ. "I always do."

CHAPTER 7

Something was wrong. Whether it was instinct, inspiration, or experience that made CJ uneasy, she recognized the sensation all too well. She quickly surveyed her surroundings. The natatorium was not unlike many indoor pools where she had practiced and competed since leaving Arizona.

The main entrance to the building led to a reception area crowded with swimmers and fans arriving or leaving. Across from the receptionist's desk lay a basketball court where athletes sprawled out on towels and sat on chairs while they waited for their events.

Just past the receptionist's desk was the main hallway that led to the pool, where the action would take place. The locker rooms also came off that hallway, and, further down, glass doors led directly into the spectator seating—bleachers situated along the length of the indoor pool.

Inside the pool area, chlorine and sweat scented the humid air. Poolside, CJ stood among some of the top swimmers in the country as the first heat of the 800-meter freestyle began. She had already completed her warm-up, and in just a few more minutes she would compete in the 100-meter breaststroke, the event she hoped would carry her to the Olympics.

In three months, the Olympic trials would begin in California, but for now the focus was here in Minneapolis, where she was one of many trying to qualify for that all-important meet. Excitement and anticipation hummed throughout the large aquatic center, but beneath it was something else. CJ continued to look around, wondering if she was just being paranoid.

She took a deep breath and brushed a stray hair out of her face. Outwardly, she looked like a typical swimmer—cap and goggles in hand, wearing a warm-up jacket over her suit with a towel slung around her waist. Yet, as she glanced at the other swimmers preparing for their races, she wondered if she would ever be typical again.

Across the pool she could see Bridget Bannon stretching next to several of CJ's former teammates. Aaron stood nearby, clipboard in hand. CJ had run into him briefly when she checked in, and he had acted as though he didn't even know her. The silent treatment was pretty consistent among everyone from CJ's former team with the exception of a few catty remarks from some girls in the locker room.

CJ rolled her shoulders, trying to ease the tension that had settled there. She felt out of place, an odd sensation for someone who had been swimming competitively since the age of four.

Though she had tried not to think about it, CJ was forced to acknowledge how much work still lay ahead of her and the almost overwhelming hurdles she faced in trying to find a new coach, or even worse, go it alone. Each swimmer on deck shared her goals, and she knew that most of them would face disappointment as they tried to make the Olympic team.

CJ thought of her father, of how he'd shared her hopes and dreams that she would someday swim in the Olympic Games. She could almost hear him now, telling her she was going to make it. If she worked hard enough, she would never be disappointed, no matter the outcome. So many times he had told her that someday he would see her walking in the opening ceremonies wearing red, white, and blue.

A sudden chill ran through CJ, and she analyzed her surroundings again. What was making her so uneasy? *Maybe it's just nerves,* she told herself. She had faced her vulnerability after quitting her team earlier that week, aware of the irony that her skills as a swimmer—which she knew could have improved with the elite team—had been her downfall. Bridget Bannon, the star of the team, did not want competition from her own teammates, and, obviously, the coach agreed.

The cheering from the stands intensified as the current race approached its conclusion. Again, CJ looked around. Seeing nothing unusual, she glanced at the spectator entrance to the swimming pool area. One of the marshals was on his cell phone, and Tara was quickly moving toward her. She was right. Danger was lurking once again.

Behind her a buzzer sounded as another race began. CJ moved across the crowded deck toward Tara. She scanned the pool area and bleachers as she walked. Her heartbeat quickened as she tried to keep her gait steady to avoid drawing attention to herself.

Her eyes were on the stands when she saw him—Jimmy Malloy, the man her former boyfriend had spoken of the day he was killed. Malloy stood on the top level of the bleachers, scanning the deck. He was dressed casually as though he belonged there in the stands, his windbreaker covering a plain polo shirt. While Malloy was known to be an integral part of Rush's smuggling organization, all attempts at apprehending him had failed.

Though no one had said it, CJ knew the FBI suspected that Malloy had arranged Leonard Abbott's death. The fact that Abbott had more first-hand knowledge than CJ did of Malloy's involvement in the smuggling ring—as well as

Rush's role in the top spot—made Abbott the greater threat as a witness. CJ had always wondered if her testimony was really necessary, but the presence of Malloy reconfirmed what the federal district attorney had told her. Rush still believed that without her testimony, he would be free.

Out of the corner of her eye, CJ saw Tara talking to one of the facility's security guards, then looking out over the sea of swimmers on deck, presumably seeking her. Instinctively, CJ's eyes focused on Malloy, still standing in the crowd as if he belonged there.

A shiver ran down her spine as she watched Malloy study the athletes making their way to and from their events. How had he found her? Had the organization paid off someone in the FBI to reveal her location, or had he discovered some other way of finding her? As a precaution, Tara had registered CJ for the meet at the last minute, but somehow she had been found before competing in even one race.

* * *

Malloy observed the athletes moving to the starting end of the pool. This was her race; he was sure of it. Once again, Malloy read over the heat sheet in front of him. All of the swimmers in the event had posted numerous results over the past season, except one. It had to be Christal Jones.

Frustrated that he couldn't identify her from the many athletes wearing caps and goggles, Malloy moved down toward the pool entrance. He was nearly to the bottom of the bleachers when CJ's heat was called to the blocks. He didn't have to check the heat sheet to know that the empty lane belonged to her.

Again he watched the athletes on the deck, this time scanning the entire area. Then he saw her. She was looking at the floor, apparently trying to blend in with a group of girls heading for the locker room. Even from across the pool he could tell she was nervous.

He had studied the schematics of the building and his men were well positioned. If she thought she could escape this time, she was sadly mistaken. Predicting that she would move through the locker room to the hallway, Malloy moved to the doorway leading from the spectator area to the main hall. He stepped through just as a hand grabbed his arm.

"Jimmy Malloy?"

Malloy looked at the man, tagging him immediately as a government agent of some sort. He figured he only needed a minute or two before the girl would emerge from the locker room doors just twenty yards away from where he was now standing. Rather than rely on the weapon beneath his jacket, Malloy opted to stall.

"Who?" Malloy looked at him, feigning confusion. "I'm sorry. You must have me confused with someone else."

"If you could please come with me, sir."

The grip remained steady on his arm, and Malloy let himself be escorted further out into the hall. The hallway was clear except for a couple of spectators and a man standing several yards past the locker room doors.

"Can I see some kind of identification?" a woman asked.

Surprised, Malloy looked at her, having thought she was just another fan. Now that he looked at her more closely, he could see that awareness in her eyes common to federal agents.

"Can you tell me what all of this is about?" Malloy asked instead of reaching for his wallet.

Before the woman could answer, Malloy saw the girls' locker room door open. Christal Jones peeked out of the doorway, her eyes meeting his. Malloy smiled and looked past her, his nod nearly imperceptible.

To his surprise, the girl turned and saw the gunman just in time. She threw herself back against the door just as a shot rang out and the door jamb splintered above her. As she scrambled back into the locker room, Malloy's gunman turned and shot one of the federal agents. The woman already had her weapon drawn and returned fire, hitting the gunman with both shots.

A scream echoed behind them as a spectator witnessed the terrifying scene. Malloy grabbed the spectator and pushed her into the female agent. In the confusion, Malloy rushed to the exit at the end of the hall and promptly headed for the central part of the college campus. He tugged his jacket tighter around him, attempting to blend in with the teachers and students.

Once he was clear of the natatorium, Malloy pulled out his cell phone to put his contingency plan into action.

* * *

CJ ran through the locker room door onto the pool deck. Seeing the crowd forming by the doorway leading from the spectator area into the hall, she froze. Her whole body trembled and she couldn't seem to catch her breath. Not knowing what to do, she felt powerless. She kept hoping one of the marshals would find her, but several minutes passed without any sign of them.

She closed her eyes, a prayer in her heart that she would somehow find a way to safety. Looking up, she noticed an emergency exit near where she had left her swim bag. Still shaking, she moved toward the exit. When she reached her bag, she squatted down and pulled out her warm-up pants. She tugged them on, slid her feet into her sandals, and slipped the strap of her bag over her shoulder as she stood.

Ignoring the security officers who told her to stay where she was, she turned away and pushed the emergency exit door open. She broke into a run as the alarm sounded and someone shouted at her.

Wind stung CJ's eyes as she raced through the narrow parking lot right next to the aquatics building and across the street into a much larger parking lot. She could hear sirens approaching and quickly ducked behind a large van. She peeked out from her hiding place and watched two ambulance attendants grab their gear and hurry inside the aquatic center.

Retrieving her cell phone from her bag, CJ pressed one of the speed-dial numbers. Doug Valdez answered on the second ring.

"Did you make it?" Doug asked, clearly aware that her race should have been completed by now.

"I didn't get to swim," CJ answered breathlessly. "Malloy is here."

Doug's voice sharpened. "Where are the marshals assigned to you?"

"I don't know. I heard gunshots." A sob escaped her. She closed her eyes, took a deep breath, and forced herself to continue. "Doug, I don't know if they're okay."

"Stay where you are," Doug ordered. "I'll call into the 9-1-1 operator out there and get a situation report."

CJ hung up as footsteps approached. Heart pounding, she dropped to the ground and slid beneath the van beside her, pulling her bag out of sight. Her body tensed as the footsteps paused several yards away. She concentrated on keeping her breathing quiet and steady, trying to ignore the cold, wet pavement beneath her. She closed her eyes, silently praying that the Lord would once again protect her.

The footsteps continued methodically toward her. CJ could hear the wind whistling through the trees, the occasional car driving by, and the last of the winter's snow crunching beneath the approaching stranger's feet.

Shivering, CJ wondered if the feet belonged to one of the bad guys or someone simply searching for his car in the huge parking lot. When her cell phone rang, she ran out of options. The footsteps quickened toward the van. As the shiny, black shoes came into view, she shoved her bag right into their path. Even as she heard the man mutter an oath and stumble to the ground, she slid out from under the van on the other side.

She ran into the next row of cars, ducking behind a sedan just as a gunshot sounded and a car window shattered. A scream pierced the air, but she didn't realize that the sound had come from her. Bending over to stay out of sight, she continued weaving in and out of the parked vehicles, praying that help would arrive soon.

The sound overhead didn't register in her brain until she saw the police helicopter hovering above her. The burst of gunfire lasted only seconds. She heard rather than saw the bullet strike the man following her. Before she knew it, two police cars were parked in front of her. The helicopter landed in the middle of the street, and CJ was loaded inside moments later.

As they lifted up above the city and the Mississippi River came into view, CJ stared blindly at the scenery below. Her body was shaking from the adrenaline rush, and she knew that the tears would start as soon as she was alone. Once again the Lord had provided her with a way to safety. She just hoped her prayers for a normal life would be answered someday.

CHAPTER 8

Matt wasn't having a good day. He had spent most of the last twenty-four hours expecting CJ to walk in the door of his St. Louis hotel room, and his anxiety level had been steadily rising with each hour that passed. She had planned to stop in St. Louis and come to his last game against the Cardinals, but he hadn't heard anything from her since she left for her swim meet several days before.

Surprised that CJ hadn't called after swimming the 100 breaststroke, Matt continued to push aside the nagging feeling that something wasn't quite right. He had tried several times to reach Doug on his cell phone, but each time the call went directly to voice mail. Matt left three urgent messages asking Doug to call him, but he knew that with his own work schedule, Doug might have missed him.

Logic told him that the U.S. Marshals were probably just being overly protective again and had decided not to let her make the detour, and he already knew from experience that Doug wasn't going to leave a message with a hotel clerk. Still, logic and experience didn't stop the worry from gnawing at his stomach.

Wearily, he made his way toward his hotel room. His team's game against the St. Louis Cardinals had ended an hour previously—a long and painful loss for the Phillies. The fact that Matt had spent most of the game looking for his wife in the stands certainly hadn't helped his performance on the field, and he had been glad to see the game end. Now he glanced down at his watch, not surprised to see that it was already one o'clock in the morning.

He slid his keycard into the lock and stepped inside, light spilling into the room from the hallway. His spirits lifted immediately when he saw the silhouette of a woman standing next to his bed, wearing a thin, flowing nightgown. Excited that CJ had managed to stop in St. Louis after all, he flipped on the light. His jaw dropped when he realized that the woman was not his wife.

Eyes wide, Matt ducked back into the hall and checked the room number to verify that he was in the right room. He looked back into the room and noticed his suitcase next to the dresser where he had left it. Now certain that he was in the right place, he kept a hand on the door to keep it open and managed to find his voice. "I'm sorry, but you're in the wrong room."

"I don't think so." She smiled seductively, moving slowing forward. "I've been waiting for you."

Wondering how this stranger had gained access to his room, Matt leaned back against the door, opening it wider. "I'm sorry, but you need to leave." When the woman continued toward him, Matt took another step backward. "Look, I don't want to have to call security."

Her smile never wavered. "Why would you do that? I love you."

Matt's stomach clenched at her words, and he could only wonder which of his teammates had convinced this woman to play such a twisted practical joke on him. The shaving cream on the edges of the bases was moderately funny when he slid into second base at the last home game and ended up with a gooey mess all over his uniform. He could even find some humor in the way his teammates had hidden all of the towels when he and one of the other rookies were in the showers after a game in New York. This, however, wasn't even remotely funny.

With a shake of his head, Matt stepped back into the hallway and let the door close between them. Certain that he knew which of his teammates was behind this latest episode, he moved down the hallway and knocked on the door next to his.

Leon Davis answered the door in the process of taking off his tie. "Don't tell me you locked yourself out of your room." Humor and curiosity laced his voice.

"Look, the joke's over. Tell the woman in my room it's time to leave."

"What woman?" Leon asked with amusement as he glanced down the hall toward Matt's room.

"This isn't funny," Matt insisted. "There's a woman in my room, and I have no idea who she is."

"I don't know anything about it." Leon shrugged innocently, but his grin remained in place.

"What do you mean you don't know anything about it?" Matt's eyebrows went up, concern creeping in for the first time. If Leon wasn't responsible, then why was the woman in his room? Matt let out a frustrated sigh, clinging to the notion that Leon knew more than he was admitting. "Nothing happens on this team without you knowing about it."

"Very true," Leon agreed. With a shrug, he added, "It sounds like you need to find out what she wants."

"You seriously didn't set this up?" Matt asked warily. When Leon shook his head, Matt motioned inside. "Can I use your phone?"

"Help yourself." Leon stepped aside.

Matt called hotel security and then waited in the hall with Leon until two members of the hotel staff arrived several minutes later.

The minute the two security guards entered Matt's room, the woman started shrieking, screaming that she was Matt Whitmore's guest. Matt stepped forward, insisting that he had never seen the woman before. They tried to simply escort her out of the room, but she refused to leave, and the security guards finally had to forcefully remove her from his room.

One of the guards winced when the woman kicked him in the shin as he pulled her into the hall. She turned to look at Matt, her eyes cold and brittle as she shouted, "You can't treat me like this! I'll make you sorry!"

Leon shot Matt a sympathetic look. "Boy, you sure can pick 'em."

"I didn't," Matt pointed out with a shake of his head. "I'm going to bed."

Once inside his room, he circled the suite, checking to see if the woman had damaged the room or his belongings. Thankfully, he didn't notice anything, but he didn't manage to settle down and get to sleep until nearly three o'clock in the morning.

He was just drifting off when his phone rang. Concerned for CJ, his heart raced as he snatched up the receiver. Expecting to find Doug on the line, Matt heard muffled laughter and a man's voice. "This is your wake-up call, Mr. Whitmore."

"Go to sleep," Matt growled at whatever teammate had initiated the call. He had no doubt that the call was someone's latest attempt at a practical joke.

He hung up the receiver and rolled over in bed, but thoughts of CJ kept him awake for another hour. He still couldn't believe that he hadn't heard from Doug or CJ for the past few days. Every time Matt called Doug, the phone rang once and then went straight to voice mail, so the sense of unease that had settled over him continued to intensify. While Matt hoped that Doug had inadvertently turned off his cell phone, he wondered if something serious had happened to Doug or even CJ.

The wake-up call he had scheduled for six o'clock didn't come until seven, leaving Matt scrambling to grab a quick shower. Since this was the third time this week that his wake-up call was late, he had to assume that one of his team-mates was behind the problem. The water turned cold within thirty seconds, making his shower even quicker than he had planned. With CJ still heavy on his mind, Matt packed up his clothes, set his shoes by the table, and laid his suit jacket over the arm of a chair just before a knock sounded at the door.

He opened the door to find a room-service waiter with a cart containing food and a pot of coffee, the latter something he clearly hadn't ordered. Upon hearing that Matt didn't want coffee, the waiter entered the room and proceeded to remove the pot from the tray, knocking it over and spilling coffee into Matt's shoe. Flustered by his clumsiness and the mess caused by it, the waiter apologized profusely, promised to replace the shoes Matt had intended to wear that morning, and promptly spilled oatmeal on Matt's suit jacket.

Matt took one look at the gooey mess oozing down the sleeve of his favorite jacket, shook his head, and acknowledged that this was going to be a lousy day.

Embarrassed beyond words, the young waiter grabbed the cloth napkin off the tray and began wiping at the jacket. Matt just shook his head and put a hand on the boy's shoulder. "Don't worry about it. Accidents happen."

By the time he convinced the waiter that it wasn't necessary for him to replace the soiled clothing, Matt only had seven minutes before he was scheduled to be on the bus transporting the team to the airport.

The elevator was out of order, forcing him to jog down six flights of stairs, his shoe squishing with each step, and somehow the bellhop managed to lose his luggage between his room and the lobby. The bellhop insisted that he had loaded it into the service elevator but that the doors had closed, leaving the luggage in the elevator and the bellhop still standing in the hallway on Matt's floor. Though the bellhop raced down the stairs to meet the luggage, the elevator was empty when it reached the lobby. Obviously, the elevator had stopped somewhere on the way down, and someone had taken Matt's luggage.

The search for his missing bag was underway nearly ten minutes before the police arrived to ask Matt to file a police report about the incident in his room the night before. The two officers informed him that the troubled woman in his room the night before had pulled the same stunt on no less than four other celebrities in the past six months.

In each situation, the woman had managed to gain access to the celebrity's hotel room and declare her love. When her affections were not returned, she threatened to expose some fictitious story of improper behavior to the tabloids unless she was compensated for her pain and suffering. Because hotel security had finally called the police when the woman continued to create a disturbance earlier that morning, she was already being held at the police station. Unfortunately, Matt's statement was needed so that the police could continue to detain her and hopefully get a psychiatric evaluation ordered by the judge.

Already running behind schedule, the team manager excused Matt to go down to the police station, ordered the hotel staff to find his missing luggage, and made a call to the team's front office to have them arrange for a later flight back to Philadelphia for Matt.

Once at the police station, Matt was able to explain the events of the night before in less than an hour. After he had identified the woman in his hotel room from the photos he was shown, one of the policemen took him back to the hotel, where he was able to retrieve his missing luggage.

He wasn't sure how it had ended up in the kitchen, but he didn't have time to ask before the hotel manager arranged for a driver to take him to the airport. The oatmeal-stained suit jacket had been sent to a one-hour dry cleaner and was with his luggage in the car. Matt diverted to a department store long enough to pick up a new pair of shoes to replace the coffee-logged ones, and made it to the airport with nearly an hour to spare before his newly scheduled flight.

Just as Matt was thinking that the day might not be a total loss, it got worse. First class was overbooked, and he was the lucky soul who got to fold his six-foot-three-inch frame into the middle seat of the back row. The man on the aisle was even taller than Matt and probably outweighed him by at least sixty pounds, most of it around his middle. The woman in the window seat had a child on her lap that was probably around a year old. The baby looked cute enough when they started taxiing onto the runway, but as soon as they lifted off, he started screaming like a banshee.

The woman tried to calm her baby down with the basics first: a cup of juice, crackers, his favorite toy. Within fifteen minutes, the boy was shrieking beyond reason, and the flight attendant came back to try to help. Nothing helped. After nearly an hour, the boy's screams turned into muffled sobs and he looked like he was finally going to drift off to sleep. His little body relaxed against his mother for a moment, right before he leaned forward and vomited on Matt's arm.

Matt just raised his eyes heavenward as the woman thrust a burp cloth into his hand and began a litany of apologies.

Matt wiped at the spot on his sleeve, choosing not to think about the mess on his new shoe that he couldn't reach anyway.

Any window of time he might have had to stop by his house on the way to the stadium disappeared when the plane sat on the runway for nearly forty-five minutes after landing, waiting for a gate. He tried to fight the concern and anxiety that continued to build about why he still hadn't heard from CJ and attempted to console himself that it wouldn't be long before he would see her. With that thought in mind, he stepped through security, smiling when he saw the driver the team had sent for him so that he wouldn't have to find a cab.

With his luggage in hand, Matt climbed into the car, leaned back, closed his eyes, and assured himself that tonight he would be home with his wife beside him. Maybe by then he could laugh about his day.

* * *

Matt scanned the seats down the first base line, nerves fluttering in his stomach. She wasn't there yet. Why wasn't she there yet? He glanced over at the friends' box where most of the other players' wives and girlfriends were seated. Many of them chatted among themselves, especially those whose husbands had been with the team for several years.

The air hummed with excitement as the national anthem was sung and the first pitch was thrown. Children chattered away happily, many of them wearing baseball gloves in the hopes of catching a foul ball. Parents made their way to their seats, laden down with the requisite cotton candy and popcorn. The weather was nearly perfect, just shy of seventy degrees as the sun began to set in the clear sky. Nothing could compare to a spring day in the major leagues.

Matt stepped out onto the field, taking his position at first base. Once again, he glanced into the stands to the section where CJ should be sitting. He could identify her seats instinctively after catching a glimpse of her at several of his games during the first few weeks of the season. Her seats were on the third row directly behind the Phillies' dugout, making it easy for Matt to spot her.

At first, CJ came with a friend from church. After Tara and Lacey showed up, they began taking turns accompanying her. Since he played an average of six games a week, he expected they were going to get their fill of baseball this season. Matt knew that coming to his games with someone helped CJ maintain the illusion that she was just another face in the crowd. Still, he looked forward to the day when she would take her place with the other players' wives.

If all went well, CJ would be able to sit there with them before summer ended. At least she would be able to sit there when she wasn't out of town preparing for the Olympics. Though CJ was full of doubts, Matt was confident in his wife's ability to make the cut. The FBI's ability to keep her safe during competition was another story.

The first two innings passed with no score. As he took the field at the top of the third inning, Matt checked the stands once again. Surely Doug or Keith would have told him if something was wrong. Even as that thought crossed his mind, he saw Keith in the stands. Matt glanced at the seat next to Keith, surprised to see Doug Valdez instead of CJ.

The excitement of the game drained from Matt as the possibilities flooded through his mind. Hot waves of fear rolled over him, and worry showed in his eyes when he met Doug's stare. Matt could hear the shouts from the stands, he was aware of the signal the catcher gave to the pitcher, yet he barely noticed the feel of the baseball glove on his hand.

The first batter struck out as Matt's mind whirled with possible reasons for CJ's absence, many of them too scary to entertain. A line drive hit right at him snapped Matt back to reality. He caught the ball instinctively, more to prevent himself from getting hit than to get the out. The rest of the inning seemed to drag on as two men managed to get on base and a third player kept hitting foul balls to prevent another strikeout.

When the third out was finally made, Matt considered how he might contact Doug for information. He was still on the steps to the dugout when the equipment manager handed him a note.

"What's this?" Matt asked the older man.

"Man asked me to give that to you. Said it was important."

"Thanks," Matt muttered, making his way to the bench as he tore open the envelope. He breathed a sigh of relief when he read the contents.

Everyone's okay. Meet you after the game at your place.

The note was unsigned, but Doug's presence left no doubt as to the note's origin. Running a hand through his short blond hair, Matt rolled his shoulders, trying to relieve the tension centered there. With a sigh, he grabbed a batting helmet and prepared to get back to work.

* * *

CJ paced across the living room of the sparsely furnished apartment, unable to relax. After spending three days in a hotel in Chicago—thankfully one with a lap pool—CJ had finally ended up in Miami with her security entourage in tow. The Phillies game was on the radio, reminding her that she would have been watching the game in person had the weekend not taken such an unexpected turn.

If she remembered Matt's schedule correctly, he would have just returned that morning from a seven-day road trip. Doug had spoken to her when she was in Chicago, and he had assured her that he would get word to Matt about her whereabouts. She had hoped that Doug would have gotten word to him in St. Louis, but apparently Doug and Matt had played phone tag over the past several days, and Doug wasn't about to leave a message of such a sensitive nature. Knowing Matt, when she failed to show up, he probably just assumed the marshals hadn't let her stop in St. Louis.

Since Matt often went straight to the stadium on travel days, he might not even know she was missing until she didn't show up for the game. Word had already filtered down that one federal marshal had been shot at the swim meet. His prognosis was still uncertain, but the surgery appeared to have been successful in removing the single bullet that had penetrated his chest just centimeters from his heart. The shooter had been killed, but Malloy had gotten away.

Tara was still on CJ's security detail, and Lacey had joined them en route to Miami. CJ and Tara had flown from Chicago to New York, where Lacey had met up with them. Then they hopped planes twice before finally ending up in Tampa Bay. From there, they had driven to Miami.

The security level was higher than CJ had seen it in a long time. Even now, Lacey stood guard outside the door, while Tara was out getting supplies for the week they anticipated staying at their current location.

Though it was difficult, CJ tried to push aside her concern for the injured marshal, instead focusing on how she might regain some control of her life. For more than two years, she had been operating under the assumption that after Chris Rush was convicted this whole ordeal would end and she would be free to live a normal life. Since the appearance of Jimmy Malloy, she was second guessing that notion. Would Malloy really leave her alone after Rush was put in prison once and for all? Or would he wait until she thought she was safe and then finish what he had tried and failed at so many times before?

Though she had seen photographs of him, CJ had never seen Malloy in person until the swim meet in Minneapolis. Had he come out of hiding because the stakes were higher, or did he think that she was a threat to him also?

Malloy had arranged Chase's murder—CJ was certain of that. On the day Chase died, CJ had heard the two men who shot him reveal that Malloy had sent them. In addition, the police had confirmed that the men arrested were Malloy's associates. Chase would still be alive today had it not been for Malloy. Yet CJ also knew, after testifying in many trials, that almost everything she knew about Malloy was hearsay. She wasn't a credible threat to him—at least the government didn't think so. That opinion had solidified over the past several months since Malloy had been noticeably absent. From the information Doug had given her, everyone believed he had left the country and set up shop somewhere else.

CJ looked out the window, grateful that she would only have to spend a week here. Two garbage dumpsters lined the alley below, both overflowing with construction materials from the building that filled her view. What would become a sleek, new high-rise currently looked more like an oversized erector set. In the early evening, the sounds of construction had finally ceased, and now darkness was falling over the neighborhood.

As Matt came up to bat, CJ turned to look at the radio. Sitting down on the couch, she clasped her hands together, visualizing her husband as he stepped up to the plate. After two balls and a strike, Matt's bat connected with the ball, sending it down the third base line for a single. The teammate that followed him at bat hit a home run on the second pitch to bring them both home.

CJ stood again to pace. She knew Matt was still uncertain about what his future held, especially since his playing time had varied wildly this season. Some games he played all nine innings, others he didn't play at all. With each game, Matt's frustration grew. Rumors that he might get traded kept him from complaining—and kept him hoping that they would be able to remain together.

CJ wondered what would happen with Matt's career now that he no longer had any family ties in Philadelphia. Tears welled up in her eyes as she thought of the emptiness the next two months would hold for her. She had anticipated the difficulty of having her husband on the road half of the time as she trained for the Olympics. Never had she dreamed that she would lose her coach, her identity, and her home in less than a week.

Even if the FBI did allow her to compete again, the thought of training without the support of either her husband or a coach was incomprehensible. Though Tara had made sure she could practice twice each day, CJ knew that she was doing little more than holding steady. She needed help if she was going to make it to the Olympics.

That morning her prayers had been full of questions, but she still felt unsettled as she pondered her future. She had tried to break down her obstacles, thinking that maybe she could tackle them one at a time. The first steps in those plans were to qualify for the Olympic trials and to finally testify against Rush. Then, ultimately, she hoped that she and Matt could begin a normal life together.

She could feel the tears threaten when she thought of how much Matt had integrated himself into her Olympic dreams. For so many years, she had practiced and worked and improved so that she might one day swim in the Olympics. Those dreams had been part of her for as long as she could remember—ever since her father told her bedtime stories and convinced her that anything was possible.

Only recently had CJ begun to recognize the sacrifices her father had made to help her pursue her love of swimming. He had never missed a meet before he died, and he had never complained about the hours and sometimes days he had to take off work to be there for her.

Her father had taught her how to work hard, how to run a household, and how to love and be loved unconditionally. When he died, CJ's dreams for Olympic glory had intensified. She wanted to compete less for herself than she did for the memory of her father and his sacrifices for her.

Somehow Matt understood how her dreams were tied to her future as well as her past. Like her, Matt came from a family who understood how to balance generosity, love, and sacrifice. And like her father, Matt loved and supported her unconditionally.

She knew that if she were to speak to him, Matt would encourage her to follow her dreams. In the next breath would be his concern for her safety. Seldom did he express fear for his own safety, but CJ felt it weighing heavily on her now.

If Malloy remained free, how could she be certain that she and Matt would be safe? The fear she felt for her own safety paled in comparison to the panic she experienced when considering that Matt could be in danger because of her.

The door opened and Tara walked through, a gallon of milk in one hand and a bag of groceries in the other. A soft-sided briefcase hung from her shoulder along with her purse.

"I got the stuff for eggs Benedict for breakfast tomorrow," Tara turned with a grin. "I figured you owed me after I picked this up for you."

"What is it?" Curiosity had CJ moving toward the kitchen.

"A laptop. I thought you might want to get online and check out when the next swim meet is."

CJ's eyes lit up. "Are you serious?" She took the computer bag that Tara handed her. "Do you think Doug will let me try again?"

"He'll figure something out." Tara motioned to the desk situated in the living room. "By the way, I'm sorry I let Malloy get away."

Surprise evident in her eyes, CJ stared at Tara. "Tara, you killed a man to protect me."

"I should have killed two." Tara shrugged and pulled a package of English muffins from the bag. "Go ahead and start looking while I put the groceries away."

CJ hesitated a moment, not sure what to say. "Hey, Tara," she finally said, waiting for Tara to look up at her. "I assume Lacey wants eggs Benedict for breakfast too."

"Oh, yeah. He said he loves anything that isn't cold cereal."

"In that case, I'll start cooking as soon as I get home from practice in the morning," chuckled CJ.

CHAPTER 9

Matt poured himself a glass of milk, wondering where CJ could possibly be. Doug's note said everyone was okay, but working his way through twelve long innings that night had been pure agony when all he wanted to do was find out what was going on with his wife.

He hurried to the door when the doorbell finally rang, opening it to find Keith Toblin standing in the hall alone.

"Where's Doug?" Matt asked, stepping aside to let Keith inside the condo.

Keith waited for him to close the door before he answered, "He's on his way to see CJ."

"Where might that be?" Matt asked, his body tensing.

"She's being relocated," Keith said simply, not knowing an easy way to break the news. "She got away, but Malloy found her at the swim meet."

"Jimmy Malloy, as in the man that had her old boyfriend killed?"

"That's the one." Keith nodded. "We're still not sure how he found her, except that he must have been monitoring any new swimmers making cuts for the Olympic trials. Her time from her first meet must have alerted them as to what name she was using, and they tracked her down when she registered for the second meet."

"You've got to relocate me with her."

"No chance, Matt," Keith stated firmly. "You are too well known, and if you suddenly quit baseball we would have Malloy looking for you along with every sports reporter in the country."

Matt paced the length of the room and then turned back to face Keith. "I can't stand sitting idly by when my wife needs protection. Whether you like it or not, that's my job too."

"And whether you like it or not, you are not an easy man to hide." Keith leaned on the edge of the couch. "Your picture has been in and out of newspapers and magazines consistently since you were fifteen years old. And that was before you became a big-time baseball star."

Matt changed tactics as the truth pierced through him. "Look, I don't know if she can handle another separation. It's bad enough that she's trying to make the Olympic Games without a coach."

"We're working on the coaching problem," Keith replied. He moved toward the door. "I've got to get going. I just wanted to let you know that she's safe. She'll have a new alias, but Doug said he's going to keep her initials 'CJ' to make things easier on her."

Matt nodded in understanding, then asked wearily, "Can you at least tell me where she is?"

"Let's just say that Doug is going to keep a close eye on her. In fact, I imagine they will be neighbors within a week or two." He took a business card out of his jacket pocket. "Here's my phone number. I'm going to be your main point of contact from here on out. Make sure you let me know if an opportunity opens up for you to be traded. I might have some ideas of which team would suit you well."

Matt looked down at the card. It provided Keith's name and phone number, but no other identifying information. He glanced back at Keith. "I'll do that."

* * *

Doug circled the block twice before pulling into the apartment complex parking lot. His flight from Philadelphia to Miami had been uneventful and, thankfully, on time. He didn't have to look at his watch to know that it was nearly midnight, yet he knew he wouldn't be able to relax until he checked in with CJ and inspected the temporary safehouse. He knew exactly where he wanted her staying for the next several weeks, but some security and minor modifications were under way and wouldn't be completed until the next day at the earliest.

He knocked twice before using his key to open the door to the first-floor apartment. Despite the lateness of the hour, he was not surprised to see that everyone was still up. He held a large paper bag in one hand, and the scent of Chinese food quickly permeated the kitchen. Lacey was currently on watch, standing by the window so he could scan the road and parking lot. Tara sat in the living room watching a movie, and CJ was sitting at the kitchen table tapping away on a laptop.

"I picked up some takeout. I figured it had been a while since you've eaten," Doug told Tara, nodding a greeting to CJ, who had finally looked up from the computer where she was searching the Internet.

"Thanks." Tara stood up and crossed to the kitchen table where Doug set down the bag of food.

"How are you holding up?" Doug asked CJ, moving so that he could see the computer screen over her shoulder.

"I'm all right." Worry showed in her eyes when she turned to look at him. "Did you see Matt?"

"His game ran late, so I had to leave to catch my flight." Doug put a reassuring hand on her shoulder. "Keith was going to meet him after the game and let him know what's going on."

"Isn't there any way I can at least talk to him on the phone?" CJ asked wearily.

"I'm sorry, CJ. You know we can't take the chance. It's common knowledge that Matt lives in Philadelphia. Now that Rush's men know that you were living there too, we don't want to risk them connecting the two of you. We already know how good they are at tapping phone lines." Doug noticed the paper CJ had been writing on, and he moved closer to read her notes. "What have you got here?"

CJ let out a little sigh and tapped a finger on the notepad in front of her. "I've made a list of the meets that I can still use to qualify for the Olympic trials."

"Let's take a look." Resignation tinted his voice as Doug took the paper from her, scanning down the list. "Several of these are on the same weekend."

"I know." CJ pushed back from the table and stood so that she could see the list. "I actually had an idea I wanted to run past you."

Doug nodded to the food. "Let's eat. You can tell me about it over dinner."

Twenty minutes later, Doug pulled his computer out of the case and sat down to work. CJ's idea was risky, but he thought he might be able to make it work. The next major swim meet was only a week away in Los Angeles. CJ proposed that she register late and only swim the 100-meter breaststroke.

If she failed to make her qualifying time, she would have another chance a few weeks later at the end of May. Three major swim meets were scheduled on the same weekend: one in Texas and two in California. CJ suggested that she register for each of the meets. If anything suspicious surfaced, she could move from one meet to another, giving her the opportunity to swim both the 100-meter breaststroke and the 200-meter individual medley in different meets if necessary. She even promised to scratch out of the semifinals and finals of the events once she made her qualifying times.

CJ's plan would allow her the opportunity to qualify for the Olympic trials, but first Doug had to make sure she could compete safely. He had every intention of registering CJ in the next meet, but he wasn't going to let her anywhere near the pool. Instead he hoped he could lay a trap in Los Angeles and take care of the men after her.

Even if Doug wasn't successful in LA, the possibility of Malloy tracing CJ through race results when Doug did let her compete would be difficult if she only competed in one or two events per meet and used a different alias for each one. Doug was just beginning to think he might be able to pull it off until he saw CJ's notes at the bottom of the page. His eyebrows lifted as he realized she had timed everything so that she would swim in California at the same time Matt's team would be there for a series against the Dodgers.

Doug looked across the table at CJ, who sat staring at her laptop, scrutinizing the online results from her husband's game. "CJ, you don't really think that we can let you see Matt in LA, do you?"

"Come on, Doug. It's perfect," CJ stated, leaning back in her chair. "We're not even sure that Rush's men know that Matt and I are still together. You can't really think that they are following him around the country looking for me."

"I didn't think Rush's men were monitoring hotel reservations or swimming websites to look for you either," Doug retorted. He shook his head. "I'm sorry, but there is just no way."

CJ just stared at him for a moment, her jaw set. "Look, I appreciate everything you've done for me, but I need to see my husband." She closed the laptop and stood up. "With or without your protection, I'm going to see him in LA."

"CJ . . ."

Before he could finish, CJ started across the room. She refused to even look at Doug as she mumbled, "I'm going to bed."

Doug watched CJ close the door, surprised to hear her make such demands. He didn't think she would really risk her cover to see Matt, but the threat alone revealed her desperation and vulnerability. The only other time she had absolutely insisted on something was when she and Matt decided to get married. Doug knew her well enough to realize that this was her way of taking control of her emotional well-being in a situation where she felt powerless.

Doug glanced over at the bedroom door and thought of the plans he had already set in motion to help CJ prepare for the Olympics. Now he could only pray that he could keep her safe—and that all of their hard work would be worth it.

* * *

Pete Wellman looked over the swimming pool wondering what he had gotten himself into. Thirty-two years ago he had earned his one-and-only gold medal at the Olympic games in the 400-meter individual medley. Now here he was, only three months into retirement, and the U.S. Marshals were begging him to help them out with some charity case.

His posture and presence still exuded the confidence of a Marine colonel, his graying hair cut military short and his shrewd, dark eyes taking in everything around him. Though a few extra pounds had tried to take permanent residence around his middle, he stubbornly fought them off by running five miles each morning. He thought of his wife at home still asleep in bed and wondered what had possessed him to make this trip.

He told himself that it was his sense of duty that had caused him to drive the forty-five miles out of Miami at the crack of dawn to take a look at this kid the marshals were protecting. If he let himself think about it, he might admit that he was intrigued by the girl's story.

His security clearance was high enough that he had been given the basics when Lacey had contacted him a couple of days before. The girl was the only witness in a high-profile case, and the man she was testifying against had already tried several times to have her killed. Pete had only read a few pages of her file before developing an intense hatred for Chris Rush.

The girl was supposed to be a good swimmer, but security had kept her from the high-level meets that would have told him just how good.

Lacey walked into the pool area, extending a hand when he closed the distance between them. "Thanks for making the time to come out today."

"I'm here. Let's see what you've got."

"She'll be right out," Lacey said.

A moment later, a female marshal emerged from the locker room followed by a slender brunette. She wasn't more than about five foot six—short for a serious competitor. As she came closer, Pete's first impression was that she should be looking into an acting career instead of training for the Olympics. She was a very attractive young woman.

Lacey made the introductions, and when Pete shook CJ's hand, he was surprised at her firm grip.

When Pete continued to study her silently, Tara stepped in and took over. "CJ, why don't you go start your workout? We have a few things we need to go over with Pete."

"Okay." CJ nodded and moved to the side of the pool. She put on her cap, stepped in with a minimal splash, and adjusted her goggles. A moment later, she pushed off and began her warm-up.

At least she's not a slacker, Pete thought to himself as CJ proceeded to swim. Her strokes were long and efficient for someone of her size, and her strength and power beneath the surface helped negate her height disadvantage. He glanced at his watch, pleased at the time it took her to complete the first part of her warm-up.

When she began a series of individual medleys, he watched approvingly. Her butterfly was solid, probably good enough to make a trial cut but not beyond. Her backstroke was generally efficient, though Pete immediately saw a couple of minor adjustments he would make if he were coaching her. When she made her turn into the breaststroke, Pete's eyes widened. She simply exploded off the wall.

Without thinking, Pete stepped closer to the side of the pool, studying CJ's stroke. She had more of a dolphin motion than was allowed back when he had competed, but he couldn't see anything of significance he would change.

He watched her swim three IMs before he turned back to Tara and Lacey.

Lacey just grinned. "I told you she was good."

"Here is the paperwork on the one event she already qualified in." Tara handed him a file folder.

Pete flipped it open, seeing that her time was decent, maybe good enough to make the Olympic team. He turned back to watch CJ and shook his head. "Her stroke is more suited to swimming the 100 breaststroke. We might want to put her in the IMs too, see where she comes in."

"Does that mean you're interested?"

Pete didn't answer, instead jotting down a few notes of instruction on the notepad he held. He tore off the top page and handed it to Lacey. "Here's what I'll need. We start tomorrow. Four A.M."

CHAPTER 10

Doug's phone was ringing when he reached his office on Thursday morning. He set a bottle of orange juice on his desk and lifted the receiver. "Valdez."

"Hey, it's Keith. I think we may have something," Toblin stated. "Rush had a visitor at the prison right before the incident at the swim meet."

"Who?" Doug grabbed a pen and a fresh pad of paper from the corner of his desk as the fax machine on his desk began receiving.

"We aren't sure, but we think it may have been Malloy," Toblin declared. "I'm sending you a fax right now with the report. The guard did say he thought he heard Rush say something about trying to find the diamonds."

"Diamonds?" Doug stood and reached for the fax as it printed out, perusing the guard's statement. "There was something in CJ's file about diamonds."

"Yeah. It's in the police report about her friend's murder in Phoenix," Toblin answered.

Doug stood and unlocked his filing cabinet, pulling out CJ's original file to refresh his memory. "Here it is. She told the police that she heard diamonds mentioned before Malloy's men killed her boyfriend."

"Has she ever mentioned anything else about it to you?"

"No, she hasn't." Doug scanned the entire police report. "There isn't much in the file. I'll call her and see if she can remember anything else. In the meantime, check with the airlines and see if you can figure out what alias Malloy is using. We know when he was at the prison, and we know when he was in Minneapolis. That should help us narrow it down so we can figure out where he flew in from."

"I'm on it," Toblin agreed before hanging up.

Doug flipped through CJ's file again. The police report listed the few words she had heard the day her boyfriend had locked her in the bedroom to protect her from the men who had barged into his apartment. *The organization, payment, diamonds.* Could Chase have seized a payment in diamonds before he was killed? And if so, what did he do with them?

The personnel file on Chase was brief; he had only been working as a detective a short time before going undercover to help the DEA penetrate the smuggling organization that was later identified as being one of the largest ever discovered. Everything in the file checked out. Chase had served a mission to Colombia for the Church, and his ability to speak Spanish—as well as his knowledge of Colombia—had helped him go undercover to determine the size of the smuggling organization and to identify the people running it.

Assuming Chase was the honest man his file indicated, he wouldn't have stolen from the men he was investigating. More likely, he would have seized evidence and tried to hide it until he could be sure that he could get it into the right hands. Since everything in Chase's apartment had been searched thoroughly, the diamonds must have been hidden outside the apartment. Surely he would have left some clue as to where.

Over the past three years, information had been uncovered revealing that Chase had not only known about Rush, the judge who headed the organization, but also about other government officials on the organization's payroll. Yet no one had heard further mention of the diamonds until now.

Doug could only hope that, despite the trauma of losing her best friend, CJ might remember something after all this time that would help them find what Rush was looking for. He glanced down at his watch, realizing for the first time why his stomach was beginning to grumble. Ignoring his hunger, he picked up the cell phone he used to contact CJ. Always cautious, the Bureau had implemented a secure link between his phone and the cell phone they had issued to CJ. Too often, signals had been picked up, compromising important contacts and witnesses.

Doug dialed her number, tapping his fingers on his desk as the phone rang two times, then three. On the fourth ring, CJ answered with a breathless hello.

"Hi, CJ. I need some information from you," Doug said, fingering the open file in front of him. "You said that you heard Malloy's men say something about diamonds the night Chase was killed."

CJ sighed, waiting a moment to answer. "I just heard pieces of the conversation. I don't know anything about the diamonds or where they might have been hidden."

"What makes you think they were hidden?" Doug keyed in on her words, surprised at how closely they matched his suspicions.

"They ransacked Chase's apartment before they left. One of them said that they found 'the list,' and then they talked about being unable to find the diamonds. The list must have been the list of names I saw. All I know is that the men sounded pretty angry," CJ explained.

"The file said that they did a thorough search, so it sounds like the diamonds must have been hidden somewhere else."

Doug flipped to a clean page on his pad of paper and began making notes. "Is there anyplace they might not have looked?"

"Not as far as I know, except for the attic where I was hiding."

"What was up there?"

"What?" Confusion colored CJ's voice.

"You said they didn't find the diamonds. Could they have been hidden in the attic?"

"Maybe, but I'm sure the police searched it after they found me," CJ replied. "What is all of this about? Why the sudden interest in the diamonds?"

"I think Rush has someone looking for the diamonds. I would prefer to find them first."

"I don't know what to tell you. Could the police have missed them when they searched Chase's apartment?"

"I doubt it, but anything is possible," Doug admitted, repeatedly spinning pencil on the desk in front of him. "Did you take anything from his apartment that night?"

Silence hung on the line for several seconds. "I was holding a stuffed animal, a dolphin, when Malloy's men showed up."

"Do you still have it?" Doug asked. A stuffed animal was an unlikely hiding place, but it was the only item that he knew of that had not been searched.

"I haven't seen it since I left Texas," CJ answered, regret lacing her voice. "I asked Jill about it one time, but she said it wasn't in my room when she packed up my stuff."

"Then it might have been taken the night your apartment was broken into," Doug said, sure CJ had thought of that too. "If you think of anything else, let me know."

"I'm still trying to forget about that night."

"It will all be behind you soon," Doug assured her before hanging up.

Doug's conversation with the Phoenix Police Department did not reveal much either. As he had suspected, the police had thoroughly searched Chase's apartment, including the attic. Because CJ mentioned diamonds in the police interview, they had meticulously searched everything in the apartment, from the sofa cushions to the lining of Chase's clothes.

Someone had to know where those diamonds were. Though Doug hated to admit it, he knew it was entirely possible that someone had come across them and never come forward. Flipping through the file, he created a partial list of all the people who'd had access to Chase's apartment right before and after his murder: the two men who killed him, the police, the paramedics, several DEA agents, and CJ. Even Chase's parents might have come across the diamonds if they had been missed in the original search. Or CJ may have been transporting the diamonds around the country inside the stuffed dolphin until it was stolen in Texas.

* * *

"Where exactly are we going?" CJ asked from the backseat of the sedan Lacey was driving. The air conditioning blew full blast to counteract the heat and thick humidity outside. Though it was only early May, Florida was already well into summertime.

Tara looked up from the map she held and pointed at the stoplight they were approaching. "Turn here."

"You're ignoring me, aren't you?" CJ leaned forward, looking from Tara to Lacey. "Not that I'm sad to leave that last place behind, but I really would like to know where I'm going to be spending the next month or two."

Tara continued studying the map and ignoring CJ.

CJ wasn't sure what had prompted the quick move, but when she had finished her afternoon practice, she had gotten in the car to find that all of her belongings had been packed up and loaded into the backseat next to her.

Her morning practice had run longer than planned, and she had been disappointed when Pete had left before she finished. Lacey had mentioned that he might have found her a coach. Since Pete didn't even last halfway through her practice, CJ assumed that he wasn't willing to take on the challenge after all.

"Can you at least tell me if I'll get a chance to practice tonight?" CJ pressed as they drove through Miami.

"What time is it?" Lacey asked.

"Six thirty," CJ answered.

Lacey glanced over at Tara. "There's a pool around the corner. We can stop and let her practice and then go get settled in."

"Just drop me and CJ off, and you can go unload." For the first time in nearly an hour, Tara glanced back at CJ. "How long do you need tonight?"

"I'd like at least two hours."

Tara nodded and spoke once again to Lacey as he pulled into a parking lot. "We'll see you in a couple of hours."

CJ followed Tara into a public pool that looked like it had seen better days. She gauged the six-lane pool to be twenty-five yards long, with one roped-off lap lane. An elderly couple occupied the lap lane, and about forty other patrons were enjoying an evening swim in the general part of the pool.

Glancing back at Tara, CJ wondered how she could possibly get a workout.

"I'm sure you'll figure something out."

"Thanks," CJ said sarcastically.

Tara shrugged and settled into a deck chair.

CJ entered the tiny, two-stall locker room and changed into her swimming suit. She came back outside a few minutes later, pleased to see that the pool had emptied.

"Why did everyone get out?" CJ asked Tara, dropping her bag next to the U.S. Marshal.

"Adult swim," Tara replied. "The lifeguard said they have it for the last ten minutes of every hour."

"Then I'd better get started."

CJ noticed the elderly couple still strolling in the lap lane, so she jumped in and began swimming next to their lane. She hadn't even finished her warm-up, though, when the lifeguards blew their whistles and the kids came charging back into the pool. CJ tried to continue swimming, alternating between swimming around kids, swimming over kids, and occasionally having to stop altogether.

Finally, after nearly twenty minutes, the elderly couple stepped out of the pool. CJ moved into the lap lane and swam for nearly thirty minutes before a middle-aged woman joined her in the lane. After two near misses, CJ finally realized that the woman was swimming with her eyes closed.

CJ tried to overcome the moving obstacle in her lane, but when the woman nearly ran into her a third time, she debated whether she should just cut her workout short. Thankfully, the lifeguard signaled for adult swim again, and CJ moved over into the next lane, enjoying ten minutes of uninterrupted swimming. Involved in her workout, she didn't notice the end of adult swim until a boy of about ten years of age did a cannonball a few feet away from her.

Moving back to the lap lane, CJ continued with her workout, pleased that the other woman had moved into the main part of the pool to play with her children. When the lifeguard signaled that the pool was closing, CJ got out, frustrated that she had not completed her cool down.

CJ toweled off and dropped her goggles and cap into her bag. "Please tell me I'll have somewhere else to practice tomorrow."

"Okay," Tara grinned, motioning outside. "Lacey is in the parking lot. Did you want to change here or just wait until later?"

CJ took one look at the line outside the locker room and sighed. "It looks like it may take a few minutes, but I'd rather change here if you don't mind."

"No problem." Tara nodded.

CJ finally got her turn in a changing stall and emerged several minutes later fully dressed. Shifting her bag over her shoulder, she followed Tara out to the car and climbed into the backseat.

Leaning back, CJ closed her eyes and gave in to her exhaustion. She thought of her husband, wishing she could at least talk to him. The threat that Malloy posed weighed heavily on her mind. Though the FBI agents had not told her, she already knew that she would have to remain in protective custody indefinitely unless Malloy could be apprehended.

Matt would be playing right now, or at least she hoped he was playing rather than riding the bench. He loved baseball so much, and she couldn't stand the thought of him giving it up for her. Instead, the best she could hope for would be to live with him in the off-season when he could choose where he lived.

Darkness had already fallen when Lacey pulled the car onto a circular driveway paved with bricks. Feeling the vehicle slowing, CJ sat up and her eyes widened.

The Mediterranean-style house sprawled in both directions from the well-lit entryway. White stucco contrasted against the red-tiled roof, but CJ didn't get a chance to see much more before Lacey pulled into the three-car garage.

"Home sweet home," Lacey said brightly, climbing out of the car.

Too stunned to ask questions, CJ followed Tara and Lacey into the house. The massive kitchen sported marble tile on the floors, glass-front cabinets, granite countertops, and a double oven. A breakfast bar separated the kitchen from the kitchenette. Next to it, an expansive family room was lined with windows, and a glass door led to a patio and the swimming pool just beyond.

"Come on. I set you up in the master bedroom upstairs, right next to where Tara will be staying." Lacey led the way down the hall toward the two-story entryway. On one side, a wide doorway revealed a game room, complete with a pool table. Just beyond the game room was a long hallway. "I'll be staying in one of the guest rooms down that hall."

CJ trotted behind him, finally finding her voice. "What are we doing here? This house is huge!"

"Let's just say it has everything we were looking for." Lacey walked into the entryway and climbed the circular stairway. To the left, another living area was furnished with two loveseats and a coffee table.

"Lacey, I've been in the game long enough to know that the government doesn't normally provide mansions for their witnesses."

"You've always been a special case." He smiled. "The government actually got this house when the previous owner got nailed for tax evasion."

"Lucky for us," Tara commented.

Lacey pointed to the left when he reached the top of the stairs. "There are two bedrooms and an office over there." He then turned and walked down the hall to the right. "Your rooms are this way. CJ, you have the one on the left. Tara, yours is the one on the right."

CJ moved forward, pausing just inside the open double doors. The far wall was mostly windows, and a balcony looked out over the yard and whatever lay beyond in the darkness. The main part of the room contained a king-sized bed, two large dressers, and a matching armoire.

To her right, a niche in the room contained a chair, a small loveseat, and a square, glass-topped table creating a cozy living area. She passed through it and found the master bathroom.

Her jaw dropped as she turned in a circle. The sunken bathtub was the size of a small Jacuzzi, and a variety of plants surrounded the bath area. The toilet and an oversized shower stall lay beyond it, and on the other side were two generous vanity areas on opposing walls. The door to the walk-in closet was open, and CJ glanced inside to find her luggage sitting in the middle of what could have been a standard-sized bedroom.

Still awed by the opulence of the house, CJ passed through the bedroom and crossed the hall to Tara's room. CJ entered to see Tara already unpacking her suitcase into the room's single dresser. Tara's room was as large as CJ's except that it didn't have the seating area. Instead, two chairs and a reading lamp sat in the corner near a window.

"Is your room as incredible as mine?"

"I'm definitely liking this private bathroom thing." Tara grinned over her shoulder.

CJ laughed. "Whose idea was it to surprise me?"

"Oh, I think we all came up with the idea together," Tara admitted. "Doug wanted us to be on-site with you until after you testify—he doesn't want to bring in a second team at this point."

"In other words, you guys are stuck with me because you're about the only ones he trusts."

"I'm not complaining." Tara set her suitcase aside and let herself fall onto her bed. "Besides, I figure with that kitchen downstairs, we should be able to talk you into a few home-cooked meals."

"You do have it rough," CJ said, laughing.

Lacey walked up behind CJ and caught sight of Tara. "I see you're working hard." He put a hand on CJ's shoulder and motioned to her room. "You had better get some sleep. Your practice is at four in the morning."

"I sure hope this place comes with an alarm clock."

CHAPTER 11

"What's *he* doing here?" CJ asked when she saw Pete standing on deck of the pool at the University of Miami.

"He's your new coach," Lacey stated simply, watching her eyes light up.

"Really?" CJ hesitated a moment when Pete moved toward them. "I thought he wasn't interested."

"You wanted a coach, we got you a coach," Lacey answered. "Now make us proud."

"I'll do my best," CJ managed, digging her cap and goggles out of her bag.

Pete glanced down at his watch and then spoke to CJ. "Let's get started." He nodded toward the pool, which was set up long course. He rattled off a warm-up that many swimmers would consider an entire workout. CJ just nodded and jumped into the water.

Throughout the first two hours, Pete didn't say anything except to give her the next portion of the workout. He set demanding intervals, and CJ struggled at times to meet his standards. Still, she pushed on, afraid of what might happen if she really did have to go it alone.

Her legs were still burning from the kick set Pete had given her when he finally squatted down on the deck next to her. "Your hips are too low in the water on your backstroke, and you are overreaching a bit with your left arm." He then proceeded to explain how he wanted her to correct the problem. Several times, CJ swam one hundred meters of backstroke, and after each one, Pete instructed her to change something else.

With each criticism, CJ struggled to try to please the coach. She wondered if this exercise was even a productive use of her time, since the 100-meter breaststroke was clearly her best event. Still, not wanting to rock the balance, she continued on. When Pete finally seemed satisfied, he gave her another set of backstroke to reinforce what she had just changed.

By the time CJ finished her workout, the sun was up, but the campus was still quiet. Her legs felt like jelly when she climbed out of the pool and grabbed her towel. She couldn't remember being this physically exhausted since she had started training in Philadelphia after being out of the water for several weeks.

She dried herself off and headed for the locker room to change. When she emerged a few minutes later, she waited hesitantly by the locker room door as Pete spoke with Tara and Lacey. A moment later, Pete turned and walked over to where she was standing.

"Before we go any further, I need to know one thing." Pete tapped his clipboard against his free hand. "What is your goal? Do you want to make it to the Olympics, or do you want to *medal* at the Olympics?"

"I just want to swim in the Olympics," CJ replied before she had a chance to think it through.

"Why?"

"Why?" CJ looked at him, her eyes widening at the unexpected question. "Swimming at the Olympics is the ultimate achievement. I want to be there, representing my country. I want the chance to compete."

"If you want to represent the United States, you owe it to yourself and to your country to be your best when you're there." Pete jotted something down on his clipboard before looking back at her. "You have to be willing to work harder than you have ever worked in your life. And you have to be willing to make it through the trials without a taper."

"What?" CJ looked at him as though he had lost his mind. "If I don't go into the trials rested, how am I going to make the team?"

"You're going to be better without the rest," Pete stated simply. "I wouldn't be standing here if I didn't think you had the talent. Now you just have to show me you have the determination. If I'm going to help you get to the games, I expect you to work toward being the best. Whether you win a medal or not, you won't perform your best unless that's your ultimate goal."

CJ mulled over his words, choosing her own carefully. "I don't know of a single person I've ever swam with that doesn't dream of stepping up on that Olympic podium and receiving a medal. I guess I just don't want to be presumptuous in thinking that I'm one of the best in the world."

"You have to *believe* you are the best if you are going to *be* the best," Pete insisted. He nodded to where Tara was waiting. "Go home, get something to eat, and get some rest. I want you to ice your shoulders for ten minutes after every practice, and no soda or junk food."

"My shoulders aren't really sore."

"They will be by the end of next week. We're not going to do the work and then have an injury slow you down," Pete declared. "I'll see you back here later today."

* * *

From the balcony off the master bedroom, CJ could see the ocean just a few blocks away. Below her, a wide patch of lawn separated the rectangular swimming pool from the waterway just beyond. Wrought-iron fencing spanned the length of the property, and a private dock ran along the outside of the fence. A white speedboat was docked there, swaying in the wake of a passing boat.

Lush foliage isolated the yard from the houses on either side so that only glimpses of the neighbors' red-tiled roofs were visible from the second floor. The lots weren't large, less than a half acre each, but the palm trees and thick shrubbery made this house feel like it was alone on a small island. From where CJ stood, she could see parts of the maze of waterways that allowed the residents of this neighborhood to access the Atlantic Ocean.

CJ still couldn't get over the house. After she had returned from practice, she had diligently iced her shoulders and then headed upstairs to take a shower. Barely resisting the urge to relax in the huge bathtub, she had gotten dressed and started to head downstairs, but the view had distracted her. For the first time in days, she felt relaxed.

Matt would love this house, CJ thought to herself. The unadorned windows invited the outside in, allowing occupants to enjoy the tropics without the oppressive heat and humidity. Determined to explore her temporary home, she glanced around her own room. She had already discovered the TV and DVD player in the armoire, and she hoped to finish unpacking after her midday practice.

CJ moved into the hallway and headed past the stairs into the upstairs living area. She glanced at the office, noting that it was sleek and functional, containing only a desk and an office chair. She poked her head into one of the bedrooms, finding it completely empty. She walked inside and passed through the Jack-and-Jill bathroom into another bedroom, which was half filled with storage boxes.

Continuing back into the hallway, CJ noticed another door. Assuming it was a bathroom, she pulled open the door, surprised to find a staircase. Wondering where it led, she climbed down the closeted stairs and found two doors at the bottom. She opened one door that led into the garage. Then she went through the other door and found herself in the kitchen. She closed the door behind her, realizing that she had emerged from what she had thought to be a pantry.

Tara looked up from the breakfast bar. "Where did you come from?"

"There." CJ pointed to the door. "Did you know that door hides a flight of stairs that leads up to the second floor?"

"Lacey said this house had personality. If you walk into the coat closet, you can pass right through into one of the guest room's closets." Tara shook her head. "Personally, if I were Lacey, I would have picked the other room."

"This I've got to see." CJ grabbed an apple from a bowl on the counter and headed for the main entrance. Sure enough, when she opened the coat closet, she leaned down and could see the doors of a bedroom closet.

"I see you're exploring," Lacey said as he walked into the entryway. "Come on. I'll show you this part of the house."

Munching on her apple, CJ followed him down the long hall past the game room. His room was the first of two guest suites, with a bathroom off the bedroom. The other guest room was slightly smaller and did not have its own bathroom, but accessed the bathroom off the main hall.

In the front part of the house, beyond the main staircase, Lacey showed CJ the formal dining room, which was currently empty. Adjoining it was another room that looked suitable for a music room or a formal living room.

After finishing her tour of the inside of the house, CJ went back into the kitchen to fix something for lunch. The view of the backyard was breathtaking, and she wondered what it would be like to live in a house with a pool. If she wasn't training for the Olympics, this pool would be the perfect size. It was long enough for swimming laps, and the yard was large enough to support both a swimming pool and a decent sized lawn area.

CJ found the pantry, disappointed to find that it contained only three cans of soup, a box of crackers, and a couple of boxes of breakfast cereal. She crossed to the refrigerator and opened it, finding it poorly stocked as well. Though she would have preferred low-fat yogurt with fruit and a sugar-free bran muffin, she settled for a sandwich. She grabbed the pad of paper and pen next to the telephone and started making a basic grocery list while she ate.

After CJ finished eating, she rummaged through the cabinets, taking inventory of the spices and cooking utensils. She added a number of items to her grocery list, wishing she could have Matt send her a few things from home. Though swim practices had dominated her time in Philadelphia, she'd spent most of her spare time experimenting in the kitchen. Somehow, she didn't think that Lacey or Tara would go pick up some whole grains and a wheat grinder for her.

Even as that thought crossed her mind, Tara walked in. "What are you doing?"

"Making a list." CJ finished jotting down the spices she wanted and held up the paper. "We need some serious cooking supplies."

Tara glanced at her watch. "We still have about two hours before your next practice. Do you want to go shopping now?"

"You'll let me come?"

"Lacey's done a pretty thorough check of the neighborhood," Tara replied with a shrug. "Let me go tell him we're going out."

Five minutes later, Tara and CJ were driving through the winding roads, Tara at the wheel. They crossed over the maze of waterways that connected the neighborhood to the Atlantic and a short while later pulled up in front of a grocery store.

Tara looked at the crowded parking lot and shook her head. "It's a good thing we decided to come today. If it's this crowded on a Friday, it's going to be packed tomorrow."

"I keep forgetting that it's almost the weekend," CJ admitted, trying not to think about the meet she had hoped to compete in the next day. "That reminds me, where is the closest LDS church?"

Tara hesitated. "It's not very far."

"If you find out what time the meetings are, I can just slip in late and take the sacrament."

"We'll see what we can do. For now, let's get this shopping done." Tara got out of the car, looked back at CJ, and grinned. "You did plan to make lasagna this week, right?"

"I think you are enjoying this job a little too much."

"Absolutely."

CHAPTER 12

"Do you really think he's going to show?" Keith Toblin shifted in his seat, staring at the panel of closed-circuit television monitors in front of him. A battery-operated fan stirred the air in the back of the van but did little to take the edge off of the heat.

Doug checked the audio equipment that tied them in with the undercover agents strategically placed around the swim meet. He put on a lightweight, wireless headset and positioned the microphone before sparing Toblin a brief glance. "I don't know."

"I really hate being in the van." Toblin tugged at the collar of his shirt.

"That makes two of us, but it beats staying home," Doug reminded him. Both of them had worked with CJ long enough that they could easily be connected to her, which meant that neither could risk being out in the open where they might be spotted. Since one of their former colleagues had been on Rush's payroll, they had to assume that Rush would know who they were and what they looked like.

Toblin leaned forward, focusing on the monitor that gave the best view of Sherri, the FBI agent doubling for CJ. Sherri was only five years older than CJ, and her youthful appearance helped her look the part of a young Olympic hopeful. The brand-new, ultra-thin body armor she wore beneath her warm-ups was undetectable, barely thicker than a standard swimsuit, and offered her protection in case someone got off a shot.

Had she reached out her arms, she probably could have touched at least two other members of the undercover team, one working at the clerk of course, helping swimmers line up for their events, and the other dressed as a fellow swimmer. The agent posing as a swimmer had free access to all of the areas of the meet, and the one working at the clerk of course would see every swimmer coming through the meet as well as have a list of everyone who should be there.

They expected that if something was going to happen, it would happen here at the clerk of course. The clerk was situated in the far corner of the pool area, and a set of bleachers overlooked the clerking area. Sherri made a relatively easy target for a sniper, and the moment she checked in for her first race would be the best opportunity for someone to identify her. Sherri stepped up to the clerk's table and gave the name of Carly Jarvis, the name CJ had used in Philadelphia. Toblin noticed movement on the edge of the screen just as a voice came over his headset.

"I think I've got something."

Doug rolled his chair closer to Toblin, studying the movement on the edge of the monitor. The man wore a lightweight jacket, and he looked like he might be reaching for a weapon holstered in the small of his back. His eyes darted nervously from one person to another.

"He's just bait." Doug shook his head, speaking into his microphone and ordering everyone to maintain their positions.

He had to give Sherri credit. Even though she could hear everything the agents said through the miniature earpiece she wore, she didn't hesitate at all. She looked completely at ease as she took a pen and signed in.

Doug turned to Toblin and spoke his thoughts out loud. "That guy is too small-time. They would send a pro, someone who would be tougher to spot."

"I sure hope you're right."

One interminable minute stretched into two as Sherri completed the registration process. She moved away from the table, never glancing at any of the agents blending into the background of the meet.

"Now what?" Toblin asked. "We thought for sure he would hit here."

"If they took the time to dangle bait out in front of us, they must suspect something." Doug thought for a moment, weighing their options. "Have one of the marshals pick that guy up. If it looks like we only have two or three marshals protecting her, they might just be trying to draw them away, and they'll try to hit her while the marshals are busy."

Toblin nodded and relayed instructions to the various team members. Doug already had the meet schedule out to determine when Sherri would become a viable target once again.

"He's going to go for her when she's on the blocks," Toblin said, studying the monitors viewing the pool. "He will know that she isn't wearing any body armor when she steps up there in just a swimsuit."

"Get CJ on the phone for me." Doug handed his cell phone to Toblin as he tried to play out a scene that would look realistic without endangering CJ's double.

Toblin dialed CJ's cell phone number. When she didn't answer, he dialed Tara's number. The phone rang only twice before Tara answered. "It's Toblin," he said. "Doug needs to talk to CJ."

Several seconds passed before CJ came on the phone, and Keith passed the phone to Doug.

"I need some info," Doug explained quickly. "Would I be able to buy one of those full body suits here at the meet?"

"A Fastskin?" CJ queried. "Yeah, there are probably a couple of vendors around the meet somewhere. Why?"

"We think our guy's going to take a shot when your double steps up onto the starting block. I need to make sure she can still wear her body armor."

"Doug, there's no way. Those things take at least a half hour to put on even if you could find one the right size. Besides, they're so tight they show everything."

"We're going to have to scrub this if he doesn't take a shot before then," Doug replied, regret lacing his voice. "I can't let her go out unprotected."

"Have her declare a false start. That way she can keep her warm-ups on," CJ suggested. She then described the process.

"That might work." Doug nodded, his focus already shifting back to the monitor. "I'll talk to you later."

Doug spoke into his microphone. "Sherri, I want you to go to the blocks like you're going to swim. Try to look a little nervous. It'll make it more believable."

Aware that Sherri couldn't answer him, he continued, "If nothing happens before you're supposed to step up, declare a false start. Whatever you do, don't take off your warm-ups."

On screen, Doug could see the subtle nod of acknowledgement. He considered himself beyond lucky that Sherri had been a competitive swimmer as a teenager and understood the terminology. He wasn't sure he would be able to explain to her what a declared false start was, much less how to initiate one.

Doug ignored the monitor where two of the marshals were questioning the man who had raised suspicions earlier.

Instead he watched the bleacher areas that would provide the best line of fire to the starting end of the pool. His analysis took only seconds, and he turned to Toblin.

"Hand me the schematics for the building." Doug reached out his hand, knowing that Toblin would give him what he requested in a matter of seconds.

Toblin didn't disappoint him. "What are we looking for?"

"The bleachers don't provide a clear line of fire, at least not without a dozen witnesses." Doug spread the schematics out on the narrow console in front of him. "Our shooter has to have gained access somewhere else."

Toblin leaned over to study the layout with him, pointing at the clerk's area. "She checked in here, and then the swimmers will walk along there to the starting end of the pool."

"If someone takes a shot at her as they are walking out to the blocks, the best shot would be from here." Doug tapped his finger on an alcove near the lifeguard office. "But that is still in plain sight, and there aren't any exits nearby."

"There has to be someplace where a shooter would be able to get a clear shot and then be able to get out of sight quickly."

Doug stood up, studying the monitors in front of him. He scanned the area on the far side of the pool three times before he realized what he was overlooking. "The lifeguards."

"What?"

"The lifeguards all have a bird's-eye view of the pool and a clear shot at everyone in the pool area. They're in plain sight, but people look right past them." Doug reached for his microphone and pulled it down in front of his mouth.

"It's a possibility."

Doug turned on his mike and redeployed the security team. He and Toblin studied the images available to them. Three lifeguards were up on the stands, one woman and two men.

"Doesn't it seem a bit excessive to have three guards up at a meet of this caliber?" Doug asked.

"Yeah," Toblin agreed. "I would have expected one, maybe two at the most."

"Think like a pool manager for a minute. Which stands would you put your guards in?" Doug pointed at a guard stand at the far side of the pool, right above the starter. The guard leaned forward, elbows on knees, watching the races beneath him. "That one, right?"

Toblin nodded in agreement. "If I was going to put up a second guard, I would probably use the one directly across the pool." He tapped the image on the screen of the female lifeguard, who leaned forward looking at the pool, her arms resting on the rescue tube on her lap. "Make sure she could help with crowd control if we needed it."

"Which would make this one our shooter." Doug pointed to the other guard, who was only partially in view. He looked relaxed in the chair, his rescue tube also lying across his lap. Doug clicked on his mike again, sending one agent to detain the guard in question, and another to verify that he was supposed to be there.

On the monitors, Doug and Keith watched their agent approach the third lifeguard. In a practiced move, the agent rested his hand at his waist, just above the gun hidden beneath his jacket. He motioned with the other hand for the guard to come down off his chair. The next few seconds passed by in a blur.

The lifeguard swung the rescue tube toward the agent, who swiftly blocked it. As the agent reached up to pull the lifeguard to the ground, a voice came over the wire.

"The manager said that only one of these guards usually works here. The other two were sent by U.S.A. Swimming."

"The female lifeguard!" Doug and Toblin both shouted in unison, even as she lifted her rescue tube.

"Shooter! Get down!" Doug instructed Sherri. A split second later, a gunshot rang out.

Sherri's body jerked and fell to the concrete floor as two agents rushed to her side. Seconds later, another shot echoed across the pool, and the female lifeguard fell forward into the pool with a splash.

"Give me a status report," Doug insisted over the mike, trying to ignore the screams of the crowd. The ambulance crew on stand-by tried to push their way through one of the emergency doors, wading through the athletes attempting to get outside. Security had already reacted and was trying to evacuate the pool area, leaving Doug's team to deal with the source of the problem.

"Sherri's okay," one agent reported. "The bullet hit the body armor. Looks like a couple of bruised ribs, but she'll be fine."

"Good to hear." Doug breathed a sigh of relief. He signaled Toblin and moved to the door in the back of the van. "What's the status on our shooters?"

"We're fishing the woman out of the water right now. Looks like we need the coroner," one of the marshals reported. "The other suspect is secured."

"We'll be right there."

Ten minutes later, Doug held a lifeguard's rescue tube in his hand, shaking his head in amazement. He had pulled back the foam rubber to reveal a sniper's rifle inside. The two lifeguards that claimed to be from U.S.A. Swimming had carried identical rescue tubes, complete with deadly weapons inside. "I've never seen this approach before."

"That makes two of us," Toblin sighed.

* * *

Jimmy Malloy sat back and watched the news. The swimming community was shocked by the random shooting at the meet in Los Angeles. Yeah, yeah, yeah. Malloy grinned as he watched the perky, young newscaster sensationalize the story and how the shooters' plan was foiled by the federal agents at the meet. Hardly.

Everything had gone according to his plan, or at least one variation of it. Ideally, the men he sent to the swim meet would have succeeded in knocking off Christal Jones. The fact that she survived was just one contingency he had been prepared for.

He had been smart enough to front only a small portion of the kill fee, promising the two assassins a large payoff after they completed the job. Now he would use the money they had failed to earn to employ a new set of hired guns. With his own funds limited, Malloy had convinced Rush to provide the cash necessary to pay for the assassins. Only a single offshore account held by Chris Rush had escaped the notice of the federal government, but Jimmy still wasn't sure how much Rush had stashed there. Only Rush's accountant could access it, but he continued to dole out money when Rush deemed it necessary.

If by chance the feds did manage to trace the money used to pay for the hit, they would only find evidence of Rush's involvement. Malloy could easily alter the paper trail to eliminate proof of his connection to the most recent attempt on the girl, leaving Rush with both the bill and the blame. With the other witness against him taken care of, she was the only real obstacle to Malloy completing the takeover of Rush's organization.

Rush's ego kept him from seeing the forest through the trees. Did he really think that after nearly three years Malloy's loyalty could survive? The best thing that could happen for Malloy would be Rush's conviction. Malloy would put on airs for a time, just in case Rush still had some stooges within the organization. It wouldn't take more than a year, maybe two, to weed them out and claim the top spot for himself.

The remaining members of the organization were already accustomed to Malloy being in charge. At this point, taking over officially was just a technicality, one that would be resolved by Rush's conviction or death. Malloy would get the girl somehow. Once she was gone, the evidence against him would be practically nonexistent. If by some miracle the cops ever managed to collar him, they would have no hard evidence against him. Framing Rush for organizing the hit on Christal would just put another nail in that coffin. Malloy could already taste the power of being on top, and he found he liked it far too much to let anyone get in his way.

He picked up the file next to him on the couch and flipped through it. While the newscast droned on, he propped a foot up on the coffee table and began reading over the swim meet schedule for the next month.

CHAPTER 13

When she got out of the pool Saturday night, CJ glanced at her watch. Since Doug's call earlier that day, she hadn't heard anything about what had happened at the swim meet in LA, and she was beginning to think they must have scrubbed the operation. She figured that if anything serious had happened, Tara or Lacey would have told her. Maybe no one had shown up in LA looking for her after all.

After she had finished drying off, Pete handed her a notebook. "Put this in your kitchen. I want you to start writing down everything you eat so I can see if there are any changes we should make to your diet before the trials."

"Okay, but I already eat pretty well," CJ assured him.

"We'll see," Pete replied gruffly. He started toward the parking lot. "I'll see you tomorrow."

CJ started to agree and then remembered what day it was. "But tomorrow's Sunday."

"So?"

"I don't practice on Sundays," CJ stated. "I'm sorry—it never occurred to me that you would plan a Sunday practice."

"If you want to make the Olympics, you need to practice every day. You can't afford to take any days off."

"I'm sorry." CJ shook her head. "I'm not trying to be disrespectful or lazy. It's a religious thing."

"Serious athletes don't have time to be religious."

"The Olympic trials are only seven weeks away. I don't have time to *stop* being religious." CJ picked up her bag, realizing for the first time that the intense training schedule Pete had planned was based on a seven-day week. "What if I put in extra practices on Friday, Saturday, and Monday? That way I'm still swimming the same number of yards you have planned each week."

Pete studied her for a moment and then shook his head. "You're serious about this."

"Yeah, I am."

"I don't want you doing more than three practices a day. You're already in the water for nine hours every day as it is." Pete studied his clipboard for a minute and then looked back at CJ. "I'll figure something out."

"Thanks, Pete." CJ let out a little sigh of relief.

"By the way, what religion are you?"

"Mormon."

"I should have known."

* * *

Matt climbed the stairs and turned down the hall to the room he had shared with his wife up until two weeks ago. Since he had been riding the bench for the past three days, he knew he shouldn't be tired, but he was exhausted. He kept reminding himself that he and CJ had been separated before and that somehow everything always worked out. He could convince himself it was true until he got home and faced the empty condo.

Her favorite cookbook was still on the kitchen counter, and a pair of her sandals lay next to the door as though waiting to be worn. Matt wondered if it would be easier if her things weren't there to remind him of her. Then he shook his head, realizing that nothing would make this separation easy.

Not knowing when they could be together again weighed heavily on his heart. Just the day before, Matt had put the wheels in motion to be traded. Quite simply, there was only one place he wanted to go: Florida.

Though he hadn't been officially informed of her whereabouts, Matt knew where CJ was, or at least the general area. If Doug wanted to keep a close eye on her, she had to be living somewhere near Miami since Doug resided there. Still, understanding the need to be cautious, Matt had let Keith Toblin step in and run the negotiations for a possible trade. Acting as his agent, Toblin could keep their objectives from being too obvious while trying to negotiate the way to their goal.

Still, as Matt was beginning to realize, these things took time.

Pulling open the refrigerator, he pulled out some leftover pizza. He put it into the microwave, randomly punching some numbers. When he figured it should be warm enough, he pulled it out and moved over to watch the late news.

Matt flipped through the channels, settling on the first one that wasn't airing a commercial. The weatherman droned on about the rain that might or might not happen the next day, citing the expected percentage of humidity, which Matt decided he'd rather not know. He watched mindlessly, sitting up a little straighter when the sportscaster came on. As the sportscaster referenced a local Olympic hopeful in boxing, Matt wondered when CJ would have the chance to swim next.

She had left behind her meet schedule, and he knew that one meet was taking place this weekend in LA. He doubted that Doug would let her compete again so soon, but he had been given so little information that he had no idea of her current schedule. For all Matt knew, Malloy had already been found and the government was just being overly cautious in keeping Matt and CJ apart until after Chris Rush's trial.

Five minutes later, the newscaster shattered that illusion. "A shooting at a swim meet in Los Angeles left one woman dead and another hospitalized."

Matt's heart nearly stopped as he snatched up the nearest phone. Already muttering a litany of prayers for his wife's safety, he listened to the sketchy details offered on the news. Despite the late hour, he dialed Keith on the phone, who answered on the first ring.

"I just saw the news," Matt stated urgently. "Is she okay?"

"She's fine," Keith assured him. "In fact, she wasn't even there."

"Then what happened? Who was hurt?"

"We had an agent doubling for CJ. She bruised a couple of ribs, and we've arrested everyone that Rush sent."

"The news said that someone was killed."

"It was the shooter." Keith's voice was even. "Sometimes that happens."

Matt took a deep breath, feeling both relief that CJ was all right, and regret for the life that had been cut short. "Did you get Malloy?"

Silence hung for a moment. "No."

"Then it probably isn't over."

"We won't know much until we have a chance to question everyone," Keith replied. "I'll give you a call when I know more."

"I'd appreciate it," Matt said a second before Keith hung up. He leaned back on the couch and wondered how his wife was taking the news.

* * *

CJ woke up early on Sunday morning, at least by most people's standards. It was nearly six o'clock when she slid her aching body into the oversized bathtub, fully intending to enjoy her day of rest. She let herself relax in the tub until the water started growing cold. Finally, she got out and got ready for church.

Tara had agreed to take her to the nine o'clock service in a nearby community. Always cautious, Tara didn't want CJ attending the church near the safehouse.

Since she had only packed for a weekend swim meet, CJ's wardrobe was severely limited. Luckily, she had packed a simple, straight skirt and a plain white shirt in the event that she was able to go to church in Minneapolis. She dressed and headed downstairs, wondering if she could talk Tara into taking her shopping for clothes.

Though it was barely seven, the Sunday newspaper was already sitting on the kitchen table along with a box of doughnuts. Tempted, she opened the box to find two doughnuts already missing. She grinned when she saw the blueberry muffin nestled in with the doughnuts. Assuming that it was meant for her, she set it on a napkin, served herself a glass of juice, and settled down to read the newspaper.

She turned first to the sports page, starting at the back and working her way forward as she searched for the box scores. She saw that Matt hadn't played the night before and folded up the sports section. It was then that she saw the headline, "Shooting at LA Swim Meet." Right above the headline was a photo of a woman lying facedown in a swimming pool.

CJ scanned the article quickly, then read it again more carefully. She was just moving to retrieve her cell phone to call Doug when Lacey walked into the kitchen.

"I see you found your muffin," he stated, opening the box to select a doughnut.

"Yeah, thanks," CJ managed, turning the newspaper so he could see it. "Do you know anything about this?"

Lacey took the paper from her and scanned the article. "Doug called last night and gave us the basic details."

"Which are . . . ?" CJ pointed to the photo. "Who is that woman?"

"The shooter." Lacey sat down next to her. "Your double was shot, but the bullet hit the body armor. She has a couple of bruised ribs, but she's fine."

"Did they catch Malloy?"

He shook his head. "He wasn't there."

"This is never going to end, is it?"

"Have a little faith," Lacey suggested. "I'm sure a few prayers couldn't hurt, either."

CJ's eyebrows lifted. "Believe me, I have that part of it covered."

CHAPTER 14

"What are we doing?" CJ asked, following Lacey and Tara into the backyard. She had intended to relax in front of the television or curl up with a book after church that morning. Obviously they had made other plans.

"We're going out for a Sunday drive," Tara informed her, walking around the swimming pool. She led the way across the yard and opened the gate leading to the dock.

"Going out in a boat is hardly a Sunday drive," CJ pointed out, already feeling sticky from the thick humidity.

"It's Sunday, and I'll be driving." Lacey stepped into the boat and offered her a hand. "Sounds like it qualifies to me."

"*Why* are we going for a Sunday drive?" CJ asked, thinking of how much she appreciated air conditioning.

"We just want to get a better idea of the lay of the land," Tara explained. "Besides the fact that we're not going to leave you home alone, it wouldn't hurt for you to know your way around too."

"You make it sound like I need a babysitter," CJ muttered, letting Lacey help her climb into the boat. She sat down on the bench seat along the back of the boat while he did a quick check of the equipment. She supposed she shouldn't have been surprised to see that he had stashed a handgun in the storage compartment near the radio. Still, she wasn't sure she would ever get used to having weapons lying around so casually.

"Just sit back and enjoy yourself," Lacey suggested. He started up the boat while Tara cast off the lines. A moment later they were motoring through the neighborhood.

Private docks adorned most of the houses butting up against the water, and all of the yards were well kept. They passed a community dock, presumably provided for those who didn't have their own access to the water. The houses varied in style, many of them influenced by Mediterranean architecture, and most of the backyards contained lush foliage and swimming pools.

When Lacey neared the ocean, he turned the boat away from it, instead checking out the other water passageways. Finally, after discovering that the neighborhood had two access routes to the ocean, he moved toward the Atlantic. The surf rocked the boat as they passed out of the channel into the ocean.

The beach nearby was dotted with umbrellas and sunbathers, and children played in the sand and the surf. A number of other boats were out on the water, from speedboats like theirs to sailboats and private yachts.

Lacey continued east toward Key Biscayne, finally curving back so that they could get a different perspective of their current residence. From this distance, they could see where both waterways led from the ocean into their neighborhood, the red-tiled roofs peeking out from between thick palm trees.

When they were clear of the other boat traffic, Lacey turned to look at CJ. "Do you want to give it a try?"

CJ hesitated a moment, wondering if she should attempt to drive a boat for the first time in the open sea.

"Come on. I'll stay right here with you," Lacey prodded.

Tara turned to look at her encouragingly. "There's really nothing to it."

"Okay." CJ stood and moved to the driver's seat. "You promise you'll stay right here?"

Lacey nodded, standing next to the driver's seat. He showed CJ how to control the boat's direction and speed, then pointed toward home. As she accelerated and turned the boat in the right direction, a thrill coursed through CJ. The ocean breeze teased her hair, and she reveled in the feeling of the sun and wind on her face.

CJ expected Lacey to take over the controls when they approached the entrance to the waterway, but instead he just told her to reduce her speed and continued to stand at her side. She could feel herself tense as the current grew stronger, but once they made it through, the ride smoothed out and she started to relax again.

She took the turns slowly, confirming where they were going at each intersection. When she finally saw their dock, she looked up at Lacey. "I think I'll let you take it from here."

"You did well for your first time," Lacey declared, grabbing the wheel as she slid out of the seat and he took her place. He eased the boat in next to the dock, and Tara jumped out to secure the boat.

"I'm still shaking," CJ laughed as she held out her hand and watched it tremble. She stepped out onto the dock and looked back at Lacey. "Matt's not going to believe you taught me how to drive a boat."

The excitement in her eyes drained as reality hit. So much had happened in her life lately, and she hadn't spoken to Matt in nearly two weeks. Despite her threats to see him in Los Angeles with or without the government's help, she still couldn't be sure when she might see him again. CJ swallowed hard and nodded at the house. "I think I'll head back inside."

"CJ," Tara called after her.

CJ walked through the door and stepped into the living room. She closed her eyes and just stood there for a moment. She tried to visualize Matt lying on the couch watching television or maybe sitting at the kitchen counter drinking the last of the milk. He would pretend he didn't drink it, of course, and then tell her about his day and ask about hers.

With a sigh, she opened her eyes and saw the beautiful house. As much as she would love to live permanently in such a place, she knew it could never be a home without Matt.

Tara and Lacey walked through the door, Tara laying a hand on her shoulder. "Are you okay?"

"Yeah." CJ nodded even as she felt tears threaten. "I'm fine."

Without turning back, she went upstairs to her room and closed the door behind her. As the first tears spilled over, she moved to the bed and sat down. She tried to remind herself how fortunate she was to be living in such a great house and to finally have a coach that wanted to help her attain her Olympic dreams. Still, she missed Matt terribly.

Swiping at her tears, she slid down onto her knees and poured out her heart in prayer. As she thanked the Lord for the many blessings she had received and the many times He had spared her life, she realized how truly blessed she was. When her prayers turned to her hopes for the future, she found comfort in knowing that, one way or another, she and Matt would find a way to be together.

* * *

Pete stood on the pool deck, his windbreaker protecting him from the light morning drizzle. For several hours the day before, he had pored over CJ's workout plans, and he felt that he had a strategy that could carry her through the trials and help her reach peak performance at the Olympics.

He glanced down at his watch, noting that it was already five minutes until four. As the steady drizzle continued, he wondered if she would even show up. He pulled out the morning's workout, glad that his wife had noticed the weather report the night before and had given him some page protectors for days like these.

Three more minutes passed before CJ walked out of the locker room with Tara in tow. CJ pulled out her cap and goggles, stuffed her towel into her swim bag in an attempt to keep it dry, and shoved the bag under a table to shield it from the rain.

"I wasn't sure if you would make it this morning," Pete commented when CJ approached.

"I'm here," CJ answered simply.

Pete raised his eyebrows, surprised by her mood. He had expected her to come in rested and eager after a day off; instead, her mood seemed to match the gray sky. He gave her the warm up, and she moved quickly to the pool.

As soon as CJ entered the water, Pete turned to Tara, who now held an umbrella to ward off the rain. "What's eating her?"

Tara shrugged. "I think she just misses her husband. They haven't been able to talk since she was relocated this time."

"She's married?" Pete asked, his eyes darting to the pool. He hadn't considered that a twenty-one-year-old athlete would already be married.

"Almost a year," Tara informed him.

"Why didn't he come under with her?" Pete asked, knowing firsthand how the government worked.

"We couldn't let him." Tara shrugged. "Her husband is Matt Whitmore."

"Why does that name sound familiar?"

"Matt plays for the Philadelphia Phillies. He's also the son of Senator Whitmore from Virginia." Tara watched CJ's determined strokes. "He's really all she's got. She was orphaned right before she went into protective custody."

Pete shook his head, his sympathies stirred as he started to understand just how much CJ was trying to overcome. "Let's see if we can shake her out of this mood."

"As one of the people living with her, I encourage you to try."

Pete studied CJ as she swam. Her strokes were still long and efficient, but her rhythm was different, most likely because of her mood. She was a solid freestyler, and with her sprinting ability, he wondered if she might put in a good enough time to make the 400 freestyle relay.

When CJ finally finished her warm-up, Pete stood over her. "You know, it's too bad you don't have any height. A couple more inches and you could probably take one of the spots on the free relay. Not to mention, you would definitely give Bridget Bannon a run for her money in the 200 breaststroke."

CJ looked up at him, surprised that he would criticize something that she couldn't control.

"What's your best time in the 100 freestyle, anyway?"

CJ rested both arms on the edge of the pool, letting her body dangle in the water. "I've never broken 58 seconds."

"When was the last time you swam it?"

"I don't know. I haven't competed in it since high school," CJ told him.

"It's too bad you aren't taller," Pete repeated. He knew CJ was getting irritated, and he wanted to wait for her to respond before starting her on her next set. He could tell she thought out her words before she spoke.

"Did I ever tell you that the basketball coach at my high school asked me to go out for the team?" CJ asked, pausing for effect. "Because I'm tall."

"Can you shoot?"

CJ blinked twice, surprised by the question. "Not really."

"Then I guess it's a good thing you stuck with swimming." Pete pointed at the pool.

She tried to suppress the grin, but Pete saw the beginnings of it. "Now that you've had your break, I want nine 400 IMs." He pointed at the pace clock. "On the top."

CJ started her next set, and Pete was pleased to see that she was starting to get her rhythm back. Even though he had only been coaching her for a few days, he could tell she was a rare breed. CJ had natural talent, and she took every opportunity to develop it with her strong work ethic. She would never be the kind of athlete that would sit back and rely on raw talent alone.

Their conversation after their first practice together had revealed more than she knew. She believed that she could win, or at least be competitive, but she wasn't so arrogant that she wasn't coachable. She would never push anyone out of her way to achieve her goals; rather, she would quietly push right past them.

As far as Pete was concerned, the fact that CJ was a relative unknown was a positive. Because the government limited her chances to compete, she wouldn't be more than a surprise in a couple of races. They would be at the Olympic trials before anyone realized that she was the person to beat.

Pete watched her swim the individual medleys, occasionally noting something he wanted to work on. The rain finally stopped, and as the sun came up, the humidity hung heavily in the air. Pete noted CJ's time on the pace clock when she completed her final IM.

CJ was now consistently making the interval she had struggled with during her first practice. Incredulous, he shook his head at the fact that she could rise to his standards so quickly. Giving her little rest, he sent her into her next set, this time breaststroke alternating with freestyle. He was still amazed that someone of her small stature could generate such speed.

When the three-hour practice ended, Pete stood by the side of the pool as CJ climbed out.

"Well, even though you're puny, I think you just might surprise a few people at the trials."

CJ ran her fingers through her hair, ringing out the excess water. "I'm not puny," she quipped lightly.

"Sure you are," Pete insisted. "You're just lucky I like to root for the underdog."

CHAPTER 15

Matt sat down on the team bus outside of Arlington Stadium. The game against the Rangers had been difficult for him in more ways than one. His only playing time had been one at bat during a pitching change, and since talk had started of a trade, the niche he had carved out for himself as a utility infielder was eroding quickly.

Just being in Texas brought back bittersweet memories, and he couldn't seem to relax knowing that CJ still wasn't really safe. They had been living in a small town just a couple of hours from Arlington when CJ had agreed to marry him. Matt shuddered as he recalled the attempt that had been made on her life there.

At least tonight's game is over, Matt thought to himself. He looked forward to getting back to the hotel and sleeping away his worries.

The bus filled up as the rest of the team joined him, and a short while later they arrived at their hotel. As Matt approached his room, he saw Doug Valdez waiting outside the door.

"Hi. What are you doing here?" Matt asked, swiping his keycard and pushing the door open.

"I'm here for a couple of days to help Jill with wedding plans, and I thought I would check up on you."

"I hope you didn't come to see me play." Matt motioned for Doug to sit down in the small seating area of the hotel room. "I'm afraid that isn't happening a whole lot lately."

"Keith is still working on that problem." Doug sat down, waiting for Matt to sit across from him before continuing. "Give us a couple more weeks. I think we can work things out the way you want them."

"It's already been almost three weeks." Matt's voice was as weary as his body. "Can you at least tell me how she is?"

"She misses you, but she's doing well," Doug explained. "She's training with a new coach, one that has a security clearance."

"You mean she actually has a coach that knows who she is?"

Doug nodded. "He's a retired marine and a former Olympian. From what the marshals tell me, he's pleased with CJ's progress."

"I didn't know it was going to be this hard," Matt admitted, dragging his fingers through his short blond hair. "I know this isn't the first time we've been apart, but it's never been like this before."

"She doesn't say much about it, but CJ feels the same way," Doug replied. "Her coach has to tease her into a good mood about every third day."

"I wish I could see her," Matt sighed.

"Actually, that's one of the reasons I'm here." Doug leaned forward. "As soon as you know where you are staying in LA next week, I want you to let Keith know. If all goes well, we will have CJ in LA sometime during your series against the Dodgers."

"Are you serious?" Matt's eyes brightened.

"She threatened to come see you with or without my help." Doug shrugged his shoulders and took a deep breath. "I can't make any promises, especially when it comes to your wife, but we're going to try."

"Still, that's the best news I've had in weeks."

Doug stood up and handed Matt a business card. "I'm actually staying in this hotel tonight, and I'll be at the game tomorrow. My room number is on there if you need anything."

"Why are you sticking around?" Matt asked, tucking the card into his pocket.

"It's just a precaution. I want to make sure you don't have anyone following you on these road trips."

"Doug, thanks again." Matt shook his hand. "I really appreciate what you're trying to do."

"Let's just pray that it works," Doug answered solemnly.

"Always."

* * *

CJ turned her head from one side to the other trying to relieve the stiffness in her neck. She was glad now that she had taken Pete's advice to ice her shoulders after every practice. She wasn't sure how much her body could take, but Pete seemed determined to push her past her limits.

She glanced down at her watch, surprised that it was already noon and Pete wasn't anywhere to be seen. Slightly annoyed, she waited a couple of minutes before moving to the pool. Every day when she walked into practice, Pete glanced at his watch as though being only five minutes early was really five minutes late. Now, just days from their first meet together, he was inexplicably late.

With a sigh, CJ dove into the water. After nearly two weeks, she had figured out the basic routine and knew Pete's standard warm-up well. She started with the long freestyle set, trying to stay focused on her stroke.

Fifteen minutes passed before CJ thought to check to see if Pete had arrived. Lacey sat in a chair near the pool entrance, but still no Pete. CJ pushed off again, moving into the next part of her warm-up.

This time when she finished, Pete stood on the deck watching her. "Are you all warmed up?"

CJ nodded, wondering why he was late but not voicing the question.

"In that case, hop out. We're going to have you do some sprints against some competition today."

"Against whom?" CJ asked, surprised that the marshals would let any swimmer near her.

"My son attends the Naval Academy, and he just got home for a visit." Pete motioned to the other side of the pool where a man about her age was swimming. "He's put in some decent times over the years and should be able to push you a bit."

CJ climbed out of the pool and watched his strokes, noting that he did indeed look like an accomplished swimmer.

"What are we swimming first?" CJ wondered.

"One hundred freestyle." Pete motioned her to the blocks. "I want to see you break that 58."

"I'll try." CJ stretched her arms over her head as Pete's son climbed out and headed toward them.

"Jay, meet Shorty," Pete said to his son. "CJ, this is my son, Jay."

CJ shook the hand Jay extended to her, noting how he towered over her. Pete was fairly tall, but Jay had to be at least six foot six.

Jay stepped up on the block that his father indicated, and CJ turned to Pete.

"How is this fair?" CJ waved a hand in Jay's direction. "He's like a foot taller than me."

"What are you complaining about?" Pete asked. "I already told you you're short."

"I don't think any of the girls I'll be swimming against are that tall," CJ pointed out.

"Quit your whining," Pete replied, his voice laced with both humor and sarcasm. "Get up there and show me what you can do."

"Oh, all right." CJ shook her head.

Not surprisingly, Jay took a huge lead at the start, leaving CJ with the daunting task of whittling away the distance between them. She hadn't competed in freestyle since her freshman year of college, and then it had been middle distance, not sprints.

Mindlessly, she pushed herself as fast as she could, her arms reaching long and pulling deep, and her rapid kick making a constant wake behind her. Still, she was unable to catch Jay.

Breathing hard as she finished the race, CJ wasn't sure she wanted to know her time.

Pete moved toward them, shaking his head. "Jay, you added almost a second since last week."

Jay just gave his dad a shrug and a grin. "What about her?"

CJ waited, expecting the disappointing news.

"I thought it would be better." Pete shrugged. "Still, 56.8 would qualify her for the trials had it been an official time."

CJ's jaw dropped. "I got a 56?"

"You got a high 56," Pete clarified, pointing at the far end of the pool. "Both of you go swim an easy 200, and then we'll try the 100 breaststroke."

Jay grinned at CJ, lowering his voice as his father moved to a table on the pool deck where he had left his coaching bag. "In case you haven't noticed, he's never satisfied."

Before CJ could respond, Pete shouted out, "I heard that!"

A giggle escaped CJ as she pushed off the wall. As she followed Jay through the water, she decided she might forgive Pete for being late after all.

* * *

CJ stood in the middle of her oversized closet and packed her meager belongings. Though she had planned to pick up a few more clothes over the past couple of weeks, she just hadn't found the time. Except for a couple of items from the campus store, CJ still only had the clothes she had packed for the last swim meet.

She didn't have to be told to leave behind all of her clothing with the University of Miami logo on it. She needed to blend in with the crowd at the swim meets and hopefully go unnoticed. At least she wanted to go unnoticed when she wasn't in the pool.

In his sarcastic, pick-on-you sort of way, Pete expressed his satisfaction with CJ's progress so far. She had to admit that he was more clever than she had first realized. He had needled her over her height, her eating habits, and even her wardrobe for several days before CJ finally caught on. Still, even knowing that he was teasing her out of her sometimes dark moods didn't diminish the impact. "Shorty" had become his favorite nickname for her, and she was barely aware that she now responded when he called her that.

She finished packing and walked through her room, glancing back as she passed through the doorway. *Matt would really love it here,* she thought to herself, wondering if she could even begin to describe the house to him.

She could hardly believe that she was going to see her husband in a couple of days. Moving down the hall she passed the main staircase, instead opting for the one leading into the kitchen. When she emerged downstairs, she found Tara already waiting for her.

"Are you all ready?"

CJ nodded. "I can hardly wait."

Tara grinned. "I don't know if you're more excited about the meet or seeing Matt."

"I think you know the answer to that question," CJ laughed.

"I'm not sure Pete would like the answer," Tara added, picking up her bag. "Let's get going."

"Did Lacey already leave?" CJ asked as they got into the car.

"He's heading up the advance team." Tara nodded. "Pete is meeting us at the airport."

"I'll just be glad to get there," CJ sighed.

"That makes two of us."

CHAPTER 16

At the Santa Clara Invitational in California, the air hung thick with tension. The shooting at the meet in LA had everyone on edge, and security had been increased dramatically. Security sweeps had been made of the pool area and the bleachers the night before, as well as the morning of the meet. At this outdoor pool, CJ could only imagine the increased potential for something bad to happen.

As people entered the facility and passed through metal detectors, their bags and purses were searched. CJ noticed the extra security measures, but she passed through them without much thought. She knew she was taking a chance competing, and dwelling on it would only make her goals impossible to achieve.

CJ held up a hand to shield her eyes from the sun as she looked around. Coaches gave last-minute instructions to their athletes, and swimmers offered encouragement to their teammates about to compete. Pete stood beside CJ, as much a protector as a coach. Over the past two and a half weeks, she had realized that he had been recruited not only for his swimming knowledge, but also because he possessed the skills needed to help protect her. She stood beside him, fiddling with her goggles as though she hadn't sized them weeks before.

She was invisible to the other competitors, CJ thought now. Pete was right that she would only be noticed if she placed in the top three. Even under normal circumstances, CJ doubted anyone would give her a second glance. Everywhere she looked, CJ saw the country's top swimmers. She had checked in right behind the Olympic gold medalist in the 100-meter freestyle from four years ago, and the current world-record holder in the 100-meter backstroke stood just a few feet away.

The media attention would be heavy during the final heats, which meant she would have to make her qualifying times long before then.

Besides Pete, only Lacey and Tara were in the pool area today. They had told her that a secondary team of U.S. Marshals was standing by outside. She also knew that they had teams at the other two meets she planned to attend over the weekend in case Malloy showed up again.

CJ was swimming under a new alias today, and Doug had already decided that she would use a different name in each competition. Only when the Olympic trials approached would the FBI step in and provide documentation to consolidate all of her qualifying times under one name.

At first, CJ wondered how she could compete in the trials with qualifying times under multiple names, but Tara finally revealed that Doug had met with the chairman of the Olympic Selection Committee a week earlier. Without revealing the sport involved, Doug had explained that he was protecting an athlete who would be competing under aliases to qualify for the Olympic trials. Doug and the chairman agreed that the FBI would provide documentation for all of CJ's races so that her qualifying times could be resubmitted under her legal name.

CJ could hardly fathom the amount of work Doug had done to help her follow her dreams. He had asked her once why she couldn't just wait and compete in the next Olympics, especially since she would still be young enough to be competitive. Now that he was engaged and looking forward to starting a family of his own, she thought he was beginning to understand.

If she followed her dreams now, she had a chance to achieve the goals that she and her father had worked toward for so many years, and a chance to move forward with her life with Matt. If she waited another four years, she would have to choose between swimming at the Olympics and starting a family. She had little doubt that her desire to have children with Matt would quickly win the battle over her dreams of Olympic glory, especially when faced with waiting for another four years. This was her one chance to see if she could really make it to the games without putting her future on hold.

As she watched some of the top swimmers in the country preparing for their races, nerves fluttered in her stomach. She tried to visualize her race, but images of Malloy at her last meet kept pushing their way into her mind. With all of the extra security, she knew she should feel safe, but doubt still lingered as she stretched. Doug had even warned her that once her times were posted, she might be identified. Of course, he was optimistic that they could get her out of the area before anyone realized who she was, or he never would have let her compete.

Throughout warm-ups, CJ tried to ignore the talk about the LA shooting, yet it seemed like no one was talking about anything else. By the time she checked in for her race, she had a pretty clear picture of what had happened. Several of the swimmers at the meet had been right next to her double when she was shot.

As they approached the blocks, CJ realized why Doug had neglected to tell her where her double had been when the incident occurred. CJ's hands began to shake as her race neared, and she spent more time looking at the people on deck and in the stands than concentrating on the pool.

She pushed aside the frightening images, instead focusing on the roar of the crowd. Today, none of the cheers were for her. She had convinced herself that it didn't matter. Now, in the midst of competition, she could remember all too clearly what it used to be like.

Paralyzed by her emotions, CJ sat down on the chair behind the blocks. She dropped her head into her hands, praying silently. "Father, please help me get through this safely. Help me do my best."

Her head came up as her event, the 400-meter individual medley, was called. For a fleeting moment, she considered staying in the chair. After all, this was the event that she was the most unsure of. She didn't have to take this opportunity to qualify, since she probably wouldn't make the Olympics in the 400 IM. Annoyed at her train of thought, she forced herself to stand. "I can do this," she muttered to herself.

Determined to enjoy the moment, she glanced at the swimmer next to her, Kristin Hart. CJ had dreamed of situations like this. Kristin Hart was arguably the best woman in this event—not only in the United States, but in the world. Just two months before, she had broken the world record in this event at the U.S. Nationals.

Forcing her gaze back to the pool, CJ scolded herself. How could she swim her best if she kept letting her mind wander? *This is an opportunity,* CJ thought. Surely she would not face a more formidable opponent than Kristin before the Olympic trials, especially since her biggest competition in the breast-stroke was Bridget Bannon. The marshals would undoubtedly keep CJ away from any meets near Philadelphia, which meant she and Bridget probably wouldn't cross paths before the trials.

CJ's thoughts were interrupted when the whistle blew, indicating that they should step up on the blocks. CJ pressed her goggles into place. Her heart pounded as she let her arms dangle by her sides, trying to keep her muscles loose as the tension continued to build. She had already made it into the trials, she reminded herself. This was just another opportunity.

When the command came to take her mark, she gripped the front of the starting block and every muscle in her body tensed. At the starting buzzer, her body responded instinctively, stretching out over the water in a racing dive. The shock of the cold water enveloped her and she moved through the water with rapid dolphin kicks. She could see Kristin out in front of her when she surfaced, but she quickly schooled her eyes on the far end of the pool. Her arms cleared the water with each stroke, entering when they were nearly straight in front of her. Beneath the water, her hands moved efficiently, reaching for deep water and pushing her forward with amazing speed. She found her rhythm two strokes into the race and managed to stay close to Kristin through the butterfly. On the backstroke, CJ fell behind, two swimmers closing in on her as she tried to apply the skills Pete had taught her over the past couple of weeks.

When she turned into the breaststroke leg, CJ came alive. She hunched her shoulders then thrust her arms out in front of her as her powerful kick propelled her forward. With each stroke she pulled away from the rest of the field, gaining on Kristin. CJ could feel the adrenaline and the power of her stroke rushing through her, and though her muscles began to tire, she ignored the fatigue. She knew she couldn't afford to give anything less than her best, and with each stroke she became more determined. When they turned into the final leg, CJ was within two body lengths of Kristin. However, Kristin then maintained the distance between them, finishing with a solid time. CJ finished over three seconds behind her.

As the swimmers finished, the scoreboard lit up with the times and places. CJ's time was the second best in the preliminary heats. Most importantly, she had achieved her Olympic-qualifying time, by far the fastest 400-meter IM she had ever swum.

Her heart still pounding, CJ rested on the lane rope and reached out a hand to Kristin. "Congratulations. That was a great swim."

Kristin took her hand and gave her a puzzled smile. "You too."

"Thanks." CJ looked back up at the scoreboard at their posted times, and could still hardly believe the number next to her name. If all went well, her time might actually be fast enough to send her to the Olympics in the 400-meter IM.

CJ climbed out of the pool and grabbed her towel from behind the block. Pete appeared at her side a moment later, her swim bag in his hand.

"Good swim," Pete said, taking her by the arm and leading her away from the pool.

"Is something wrong?" CJ asked when she saw Tara heading toward them.

"After you cool down, we're going to take off," Pete stated casually.

CJ studied him for a moment, relieved that there didn't seem to be any urgency as they walked. When they moved to the parking lot, CJ noticed that she was being shielded, with Pete and Lacey walking on either side of her and Tara directly in front of her.

When they finally got out to the rental car, Lacey turned to her. "The media is already setting up for this afternoon's races. We can't take a chance of keeping you here."

As soon as they were all in the car, Tara added, "Doug said that they have cleared the meet in Texas, so that's where he wants you to swim your 100 freestyle and hopefully the 200 IM."

"Am I still going to swim the 100 breaststroke?" CJ asked anxiously. "I'll give up the other two races for the breaststroke."

"We'll see how everything shapes up at this next meet," Tara replied quietly.

* * *

Pete stood on the deck of the natatorium on the Texas A&M campus, soaking in the atmosphere. The beautiful facility featured an eight-lane Olympic-sized pool flanked by spectator seating that could accommodate over a thousand people. The diving well on the far end of the competition pool doubled as a warm-up pool.

Throughout the day, the spectators at the pool had grown progressively louder. Though many of the seats had remained empty for the early preliminary races, the crowd grew as the end of the preliminaries approached. The final heats were next. CJ was already in the pool warming up for her second race of the day, the 200-meter individual medley. Just watching her, Pete could feel the anticipation build. Her freestyle was classic, perfect arm strokes with a long reach and a powerful underwater pull. The wake that followed behind her as she crossed in front of him sent a ripple of excitement straight through him.

Pete knew that CJ could win the 100 freestyle today, and he was debating whether he should let her try. He was starting to think that she needed to remember what it felt like to be on the medal stand. Though he had only coached her for a short time, Pete knew that CJ's focus had been on achieving qualifying times since she had started training in Philadelphia nearly a year before. He thought perhaps her ego could use the boost a medal would give her. She had posted the fastest time in the preliminaries, and though she had obtained her qualifying time, he was sure she could improve on it.

When he saw CJ switch to breaststroke, he had to fight back a grin. It wouldn't do for a coach to look overconfident, especially with a swimmer who needed to keep a low profile. Still, his lips curved up slightly as he watched her hands pull uniformly through the water, her knees dropping deep before her feet whipped out and around to push her forward into a long, steady glide.

She was at home in the water, just as he had been so many years ago when training had kept him in the pool nearly ten hours a day. He wondered if she too felt that comfortable sensation come over her the minute she smelled chlorine or when the water surrounded her each time she dove into the pool.

CJ climbed out of the water, took a minute to towel off, and then walked over to her coach.

"Are you ready?" Pete asked, casually estimating that she still had another ten minutes until her race.

"I hope so." CJ nodded.

"Don't let these big girls intimidate you," Pete remarked, a hint of sarcasm in his voice. "Just stick with them until the breaststroke leg of the race. Then show them who's boss."

CJ lifted an eyebrow and looked up at him. "I'm not short."

Pete leaned closer, challenge gleaming in his eyes. "Prove it."

She just handed him her towel and grinned. "See you in a few minutes."

Pete just nodded and watched her go.

CJ was still grinning when she checked in at her lane. She glanced at the girls on either side of her, each of them several inches taller than she was. Out of the corner of her eye, she noticed Pete move closer to the competition pool. As he looked at her competition, his raised eyebrows all but shouted "Shorty!" across the pool.

She didn't even notice how relaxed and loose she felt as she stepped onto the block, waited for the buzzer, and began her race. To her surprise, she entered the water even with the field, despite the height advantage of most of her competitors. Thinking of her 400 IM just the day before, CJ pushed herself in the butterfly, anticipating that she would lose ground on the backstroke leg of the race.

Her backstroke felt smoother than it had just the day before, and CJ worked her way through her weakest stroke. As she crossed under the flags and anticipated turning into the breaststroke, her excitement grew. When she made her turn, she rolled her eyes to either side, surprised to find that she led the race. Afraid that another swimmer might be right behind her, she refused to look back.

She could hear Pete's instructions running through her head as she made the turn into freestyle. *Kick, reach, finish hard.* Her hand slammed into the timing pad, and she looked up to see her time. Her jaw dropped when she saw the time posted. It not only shattered her personal best, but it was a full five seconds below the qualifying time for the Olympic trials. CJ wondered if the time could be an error, but then she looked around and saw the closest swimmer just reaching the finish.

As soon as the rest of the women completed the race, CJ climbed out of the pool and headed straight for Pete. He gave her a shrug as he handed her towel to her. "Not bad."

Still stunned by her time, CJ smiled. "From you, I'll take that as a compliment."

"Go cool down. You only have about an hour until the finals for the 100 freestyle."

She raised her eyebrows. "I'm swimming in the finals?"

He gave her a curt nod. "Doug said they haven't had any security concerns here. Besides, it's about time you bring home some souvenirs."

"I think I'd like that." CJ nodded excitedly. Then she headed for the warm-up pool, oblivious to the fact that for the first time in months she actually felt normal.

CHAPTER 17

CJ rested her eyes, trying to ignore the turbulence as the plane began its descent to the San Diego airport. She rolled her shoulders as she tried to relax in the first-class section of the airplane. She had flown coach on her way to the meet at Texas A&M, and she was grateful Doug had upgraded their San Diego flight.

The plane jolted once again as they descended through the clouds, and CJ looked out the window at the city lights below. She wasn't sure what time it was, and she didn't want to think about the hour-long drive they had to make tonight before she could crawl into bed.

It hardly seemed possible that she had left the West Coast only twenty-four hours before. Though her body was weary from traveling, at least she had the satisfaction of knowing she already had Olympic-qualifying times in both the 100-meter freestyle and the 200-meter individual medley. She still couldn't believe her times. As stunned as she had been by her 200-IM time, her freestyle time surprised her even more—just a fraction over 55 seconds.

Her final race in Texas had gone without incident, except for the photographer who had snapped her picture after she took the gold medal in the 100-meter freestyle. CJ still felt bad about that man's camera; it had sunk like a stone when it splashed into the pool. She wasn't sure how Tara had managed to get the camera strap to break, but she knew better than to ask.

Tomorrow she would attempt to qualify in her final event, the 100-meter breaststroke. As the plane touched down, CJ breathed a sigh of relief. Just one more day and she would be able to concentrate on training for the Olympic trials. No more worrying about Rush or Malloy finding her. No more stressful qualifying races. Furthermore, after finishing her event at the meet in Mission Viejo, she would spend the next three days with her husband in LA—at least part of the time.

Matt and his team would fly into Los Angeles early the next morning for a three-game series against the Dodgers. CJ even had tickets for one of the games, and she looked forward to relaxing for a few days—or, rather, a few hours between practices—before focusing again on training for the Olympics.

Pete had arranged for practice time each day while she was in California, but that seemed a small price to pay for some time with her husband.

In the seat next to her, Tara checked her watch. The instant the fasten seat belt sign turned off, Tara jumped out of her seat and grabbed their bags from the overhead compartment. "Let's go."

CJ knew she should be used to special treatment by now, but she was still amazed by the way she was shepherded off the plane through the rear service exit before the main doors were opened for the rest of the passengers. She and Tara descended a set of moveable metal stairs down to the tarmac. Once on the ground, she only had to take a dozen steps to reach the car waiting for them.

The car pulled away from the airplane before any of the other passengers were permitted to deplane. Within minutes they were clear of the airport, negotiating their way out of San Diego.

CJ didn't know what time they finally made it to the hotel in Mission Viejo, but she slept like a stone the moment her head hit the pillow. She woke early, her body still not quite sure what time zone she was in.

Everything seemed normal enough as she grabbed a bite to eat and drove over to the meet with Pete and Tara. When they arrived, however, she immediately noticed the extra security. Not just the security for the facility and the meet, but extra security for her.

She recognized three U.S. Marshals in the shade near the registration table, and Keith Toblin from the FBI was hovering near the entrance to the pool. No one had alerted her to any perceived danger at this meet, yet something was clearly amiss. CJ turned to the marshal beside her. "Did I forget anything?"

Already identifying the other marshals, Tara asked, "Do you have your cell phone?"

Realizing Tara probably wondered if there was a message from Doug on her phone, CJ reached into her swim bag and retrieved it. After checking for messages, she turned back to Tara. "Yeah, but there aren't any messages."

Sensing their concern, Pete put a hand on CJ's shoulder and looked at Tara. "I'll get her checked in."

Tara nodded and moved away from the entrance to check on the reason for the extra personnel.

Despite the nerves fluttering in her stomach, CJ methodically completed the check-in process with Pete's help. They were heading for the pool area when Tara pulled them aside.

"There's nothing to worry about," she assured them. "Doug is just being cautious."

"Would you tell me if I should worry?" CJ asked warily.

"Probably not," Tara admitted. "But in this case, it's true. Besides, it's our job to cover you. We haven't let you down yet."

CJ nodded, appreciating the validity of Tara's statement while trying not to remember how many times Rush's men had gotten too close for comfort. Pushing aside the fact that somebody wanted her dead, CJ found an open space on deck and began stretching. A few minutes later, Pete sent her to the competition pool to warm up.

Three guys stood in the water in the lane next to her, chatting away as though there was nothing better to do as the sun rose steadily in the sky. On the other side of her, a girl held onto the edge of the pool listening to her coach's instructions.

CJ pushed off and started her warm-up. She had only finished three hundred meters when she approached the wall to do her turn and found the wall hidden behind bodies. She pulled up short and lifted her head, waiting for the swimmers to clear the way. Apparently unaware of CJ's presence, the four new arrivals continued their conversation while effectively blocking the wall.

Frustrated, CJ reversed direction and began swimming the other way without the benefit of a wall to push off of. The pool got even more crowded until she finally gave up, planning to warm up right before her race. Climbing out of the pool, CJ passed one marshal as she went into the locker room. Tara was just inside the locker room door surveying the athletes as they came and went.

By the time CJ proceeded to warm up for the preliminaries of the 100-meter breaststroke, she felt smothered by the extra security. She managed to find a lane in the warm-up pool with only three people in it, but she struggled to settle down and concentrate on the upcoming race. Stress continued to build, and for once swimming didn't diminish its effect.

When CJ finally reported behind the blocks, she just wanted the whole thing over. She reached one arm across her chest, trying to relieve some of the tension, then repeated the process with her other arm. When she glanced at the swimmer to her left, she noticed the girl two lanes down staring at her, a glimmer of recognition in her eyes. CJ returned her stare for a moment, wondering why she looked familiar.

Suddenly she placed the face, and she quickly averted her eyes back to the pool. The girl staring at her was Allison Harris, who had been expected to win the 100-meter breaststroke in the high school state championships during their senior year. Instead, CJ had captured the gold medal, edging out Allison by only a few hundredths of a second.

CJ swallowed hard, barely aware of the race just finishing. *Allison can identify me,* she thought numbly. They had been rivals throughout high school as well as in year-round swimming. CJ glanced up at the scoreboard. The huge, black display board illuminated the lane number and name of each contestant, and then their time when the race ended. In just moments, CJ's alias would be displayed in lights for everyone—including Allison—to see. Would Allison notice that CJ was not using her own name?

Questions continued to run through CJ's mind as the score board was cleared and the names for the upcoming heat were listed. What should she do if Allison approached her after they swam? Could the marshals get her out of the building quickly enough?

The heat before them cleared the pool, and CJ fumbled with her goggles as she moved to the starting block. She glanced over at Allison once more, just in time to see her study the scoreboard and then glance questioningly in CJ's direction. CJ looked out over the pool, quickly pressing her goggles into place as the whistle signaled for the swimmers to step onto the blocks.

Her mind raced even as she took her starting position, balancing on the balls of her feet as she prepared to spring forward. Struggling to steady her breathing, she tried to force Allison from her mind. The starter held them in the starting position a second longer than expected, and CJ rocked forward a moment to soon. She tried to stop her momentum unsuccessfully. Unable to regain her balance, she fell off of the block, opening her body into a simple dive.

The other swimmers remained on the blocks, looking down at CJ. It was over; her false start disqualified her, removing any opportunity to qualify for the 100-meter breaststroke in this meet. Banking down on the swirl of emotions trying to surface, CJ stroked to the side of the pool and pulled herself out as the referee approached to officially inform her that she was disqualified.

When Pete appeared with her swim bag, CJ had barely pulled her sweats on. He didn't say anything, but CJ could feel his disappointment. They had worked so hard, and now . . . She couldn't even finish the thought before Lacey and Tara appeared and whisked her away from the starting area and out a side gate.

"What's wrong?" CJ managed as tears threatened.

"Just a precaution," Tara answered calmly. "There's no reason to keep you here now that you're done."

"One of the girls there knows me," CJ stated in a trembling voice.

"We were afraid of that," Tara replied.

"You knew?" CJ asked incredulously. "Why didn't you do something? You could have at least warned me."

"We were told that she had pulled out of the meet because of an injury," Tara explained matter-of-factly.

"I think she figured out my alias on the scoreboard," CJ retorted, frustration evident in her voice.

"Don't worry. She'll probably just assume someone made a mistake typing in your name," Tara suggested. "And since you false started, she won't even see your name on the results. You solved the problem without even knowing it."

CJ stopped walking. "My name will still be listed. It will be even more obvious now, since I'll be the only DQ."

Tara sighed and put an arm around CJ's shoulders. "It's probably not a big deal. It's not like she shouted out your name or anything. Besides, when we realized Allison had shown up, we kept a close eye on her."

"But what if she goes out and tells everyone I was here?"

"CJ, I doubt she would go to the media with the fact that you used an alias. Besides, Malloy and his thugs already know you're doing that. By the time Allison got to a reporter, you'd be long gone anyway. And remember, we use a different alias at every meet."

"I'm sorry. I know I'm probably just being paranoid," CJ said, breathing in deeply. She didn't want to think about why she had to be cautious. When she considered how many times Rush and Malloy had tried to kill her, she felt like she might drown from her own fears. What could she have done if Allison had called out her name or brought attention to her at the meet? The wrong people could have identified her too easily. With another deep breath, she realized that Allison probably wouldn't have made a big deal about knowing her, even if her protectors hadn't whisked her away.

"Don't worry about it," Tara said, breaking into CJ's thoughts. "It's better to be paranoid than sorry." Giving CJ a squeeze, she flipped open her cell phone. "Toblin, you've got some work to do. Just to be safe, let's make sure no one figures out CJ was here."

CJ listened to Tara's side of the conversation, hopeful that Toblin could work a miracle. After witnessing firsthand the photographer's misfortune in Texas, she didn't doubt that her entry card would somehow mysteriously disappear so that all record of her presence would be eliminated. She doubted that her name on the results would cause a problem, but by eliminating that possibility, at least Rush's men wouldn't have a starting point from which to track her down.

She could just envision Toblin walking up to the scorer's table, probably wearing the standard white shirt and pants that all of the referees and judges wore. He would insist that he needed to double check her disqualification. Then he would pick up her entry card and walk away as though to go confer with the head referee. Undoubtedly he would just keep walking out of the building, taking the evidence with him.

She smiled when she thought of Toblin impersonating a swimming official. But when they arrived at the car, the reality of her situation came crashing in on her once again.

She dropped her head into her hands as the first tear spilled over. After all of her planning and training, she had blown her one chance to qualify in her best event, the event she was the most optimistic about swimming in the Olympics. With only six weeks left until the Olympic trials, she was running out of opportunities.

Although there were still a couple of big meets in which she could compete, talking Doug into allowing her to do so was another matter. Would Rush's men connect the dots and figure out that she was using several aliases?

"I can't believe I blew it." CJ shook her head as tears continued to fall.

"Kid, there's one thing I have known about you from the start," Tara said as they merged onto the freeway. "You don't do anything the easy way."

"You can say that again," Pete agreed, the gruffness in his voice more soothing than kind words would have been.

CJ looked up, her tears slowing as her lips quirked up. "Do you think Doug will let me try again?"

"We'll talk him into it," Tara assured her. "Besides, I like a challenge."

CHAPTER 18

Wyatt Murphy strolled down the hallway of the elegant Pasadena hotel, then entered his room using a keycard. He dropped his luggage on the bed and moved straight to the window, grinning at the view. *This is perfect,* he thought to himself, pleased at his good fortune.

Murphy considered himself beyond lucky to have wheedled the necessary information out of one of the hotel clerks. Now he knew the layout of the building across from him, and he knew the room number of his victims. Security at the hotel was fairly efficient, and Murphy had approached three different front-desk clerks before he found one willing to cooperate.

Like many in his field, Murphy was adept at using human nature to get the facts he wanted. He had mastered the art of gossip, dropping a tidbit of information so that his informant would reveal the rest. On other occasions, he had to rely on his charm, and sometimes he fell back on the easiest method: cold, hard cash.

Murphy also appreciated his ability to blend in. He was average in height and build, and he kept his dark hair short. When he maintained his clean-shaven look, he could blend in at most high-society functions without a second glance. Of course, when it served his purposes, he could just as easily sport a mustache and shaggy beard to give him a seedier look.

After taking a few minutes to identify the window belonging to his targets, Murphy moved back across the room. He pushed aside his suitcase and flipped open the hard-sided case that contained the tool of his livelihood. All it would take was one perfect shot, and he could move into the big time.

He froze when he noticed movement behind one of the curtains in his victims' room. Seeing it was just a maid preparing the room, Murphy pulled up a chair and settled in for a long wait.

* * *

Security was tighter than Matt had seen it in a long time. He spotted one undercover agent in the parking lot and two more in the hotel lobby. That didn't include the hotel security personnel that were present because of the team's arrival. Matt entered the elevator with several of his team-mates, realizing that he had two hours before the team would have to leave for Dodger Stadium for their first game. He found his room, inserted the electronic key, and was only two steps inside the door when he realized someone had been there.

The ice bucket was full of partially melted ice, and one of the water glasses had been used. A paperback novel had been tossed on the king-sized bed, while a pair of women's sandals lay haphazardly just inside the door. For a moment, Matt worried that he had been given the wrong room—or, even worse, that he would have a repeat of the incident in St. Louis—then he noticed the curtains billowing in the breeze by the balcony door.

CJ was sitting on a lounge chair on the balcony, a notebook in one hand and a pen in the other. One foot was tapping, apparently to the beat of music coming through the earpieces of her iPod. It was then that Matt realized she couldn't hear him.

For several moments he just stood at the door watching her. The wind teased her sable hair, strands of it dancing in the breeze. Her normally fair skin was a shade darker than usual. She looked content, though he knew better, since Doug had already told him about her failure to qualify in her favorite event.

He opened the screen door and stepped onto the balcony just as she turned. An instant later her notebook was on the floor.

"Matt!" She started toward him even as he moved to embrace her.

He felt her tremble, and he knew that she was fighting back tears. His own throat closed up, and he didn't trust his voice to speak. Instead he just breathed her in, taking comfort in the familiar scent of her raspberry shampoo and the lingering smell of chlorine she could never completely eliminate from her hair.

Clinging to one another, they stood in silence until Matt finally leaned back to look into his wife's face. He wiped away a tear that had escaped and caressed her cheek. She looked vulnerable again, and he hated knowing that she had been forced to face her fears alone over the past few weeks.

His voice was husky when he finally spoke. "I missed you."

"I'm so glad you're here."

"Me too." Matt closed the distance between them, and his lips found hers. He kissed her slowly, tenderly, offering and accepting comfort at the same time. He could feel the tension subside as her fingers curled into the soft cotton of his shirt.

He drew back and watched CJ's troubled gray eyes flutter open. He skimmed his hands down her arms, linking his fingers with hers.

"How are you doing?" Matt asked, taking a step back so he could see her clearly.

CJ shrugged. "Okay, I guess, considering that I completely messed up."

"Nobody's perfect, CJ."

"I don't have enough chances not to be," CJ insisted.

"You need to just forget about that meet. Concentrate on the events you did qualify in."

"Every time I close my eyes, I feel myself falling into that pool." CJ shook her head. "It's like I can't stop reliving it."

"Maybe I should help you think about something else." A smile spread slowly across his face, his eyes sparking with mischief.

CJ tightened her grip on his hands. "Don't even think about it."

His grin widened and he managed to free one hand, but she blocked him before he could tickle her. "Think about what?"

"You are not going to tickle me," she declared, humor lacing her voice.

Matt evaluated the situation for about two seconds, pleased that her mood had improved. "Okay," he said. "I'm not going to tickle you."

A myriad of expressions crossed her face, from disbelief to cautious acceptance. The moment she relaxed, he scooped her into his arms. She squealed in surprise, her arms automatically encircling his neck. "You're crazy."

Matt gave her a quick, teasing kiss. "Definitely," he said laughingly. "But you love me anyway."

"Yeah, I do," CJ agreed as he carried her into the room.

* * *

Stifling a yawn, Matt fumbled with his hotel keycard. He slid it into the lock twice before the lock clicked open. He rolled his shoulders as he stepped inside the room, wincing from the pain in his side where he had come down hard diving for a ball. He didn't notice that the lights were still on in the room until he was several steps inside.

He moved to the bed, smiling when he saw the figure curled under the blankets. Quietly, he moved closer, kneeling down next to his wife. In one hand she held onto the comforter, tucking it under her chin for warmth. She looked so peaceful sleeping in his bed.

Soon, he told himself, they would be together. One way or another, he was determined to be with her before the summer was over. He hated being away from her, even for a day. Before she had been relocated, she had teased him that he was overprotective. Now he had come to need her more than he had ever thought possible.

He reached out a hand and brushed her hair from her cheek. She stirred slightly when he kissed her. Her eyelids fluttered and then she settled back into a deep sleep. Experience told him that a hurricane could pass directly over them and CJ would sleep right through it.

Exhausted both emotionally and physically, Matt slid into bed and wrapped a proprietary arm around her waist. Moments later he was sound asleep too.

* * *

Ring. Ring. Ring. Blurry eyed, Matt spotted the phone on the bedside table and plucked up the receiver. "Hello?"

A cheerful voice came over the line. "This is your wake-up call, Mr. Whitmore."

"What time is it?"

"Four thirty, sir."

"Why would I want to get up at four thirty?" Matt rubbed the sleep from his eyes. Movement next to him in the bed reminded him of the reason for such an early call. "Never mind," he muttered and hung up.

"Four thirty?" Matt asked groggily, flopping back onto the bed.

"Hi, honey." CJ grinned at him and gave him a smacking kiss on his cheek. He looked up at her, half annoyed that she could look so cheerful at this hour.

"Did you have to schedule practice for this early in the morning?"

"I have to take what I can get." She climbed out of bed and picked up her swim bag. "Go back to sleep. I'll be back in a couple of hours. Maybe I'll even pick up some breakfast on my way back."

"Krispy Kreme doughnuts," Matt mumbled, promptly rolling over and sliding back into unconsciousness.

CJ smiled. She had tried to wait up for him the night before. After watching the first three innings of his game on television, she realized that she was never going to make it. Early-morning swim practices just didn't agree with late-night games.

Sliding her swim bag over her shoulder, she headed for the front door. She peeked out into the hall, grateful to find it empty except for the dark-haired U.S. Marshal standing a few yards away. He moved forward to escort her downstairs as she slipped out the door. Together they headed for the stairwell and made their way outside. Lacey was already waiting in the car when they emerged from the hotel.

"Did you draw the short straw again?" CJ asked when she climbed into the car.

Lacey raised an eyebrow. "I didn't even have time for a cup of coffee."

"That stuff's bad for you anyway," CJ retorted. "Tell you what. I'll buy you a nice glass of milk when we stop for breakfast on the way back."

"Stop where?"

CJ lowered her voice when she saw Pete approaching the car. "Krispy Kreme."

"Now you're talking."

* * *

The FedEx packages were addressed and stacked on the dresser in his hotel room. Wyatt Murphy debated whether to seal the oversized envelopes and ship them out now, or if he should try to add a bit more weight first. The fees he would collect for his latest success would undoubtedly pay for a nice, extended vacation in a place with warm beaches and cold water.

His hand rested patiently on the camera that hung from his neck. He tried not to think of how much time he spent waiting around for just a few seconds worth of photography. Murphy sighed. That was the nature of the job.

"Paparazzi" sounded so ugly to most people, yet those same people were the reason he was still employed. Just give them a good picture and a teasing headline, and they couldn't help themselves. They would snatch those tabloids off the stands faster than they could print them.

He imagined these latest prints would sell quite a few copies. Murphy exhaled slowly. The thought of taking a little time off was so tempting, but if he tapped into that well of patience he used so often in staking out a subject, he knew that he might get lucky again. Then he would use his fine art of negotiating to secure a bonus that could tempt him to consider an early retirement. Wyatt weighed his options for a few minutes more. As he calculated his fees from the tabloids and the bonus he planned to receive, he expected he could pad his bank account enough that he could give up the hours of waiting in shadows at all hours of the day and night.

Copies of his most recent prints were spread out on the table, and he grinned at his good fortune. Could he get so fortunate again? Glancing at the stack of envelopes, Wyatt grabbed his camera. It wouldn't hurt to sit on those photos for a couple of days. After all, maybe lady luck wasn't quite done smiling on him.

CHAPTER 19

When CJ and Lacey found their seats in Dodger Stadium, the first inning was just starting. CJ's second practice of the day had run late, her concession to Pete for allowing her to take the afternoon and evening off.

Matt was already hard at work, fielding a line drive for the first out of the inning and then stretching for a throw from the third baseman that was just a little too late to make another out. The center fielder caught a long fly ball for the second out, and the pitcher managed a strikeout for the third.

Matt had started the last couple of games at first base while the starting first baseman recovered from a minor hamstring pull. The newscasters had keyed in more than a week before that management was in the process of trading Matt.

When CJ had asked Matt about the trade situation, his answer had been uncharacteristically vague. CJ wasn't sure if he really didn't know anything or if he just hadn't wanted to spend what little time they had talking about something uncertain. She hoped and prayed that whatever happened with his career might enable them to be together again.

She had already come to terms with the fact that they would have to live apart until after Rush's trial and possibly beyond. Though she couldn't imagine what life would be like without the hours of training each day, she saw the Olympics as not only that magic moment when her childhood dreams could come true, but also the turning point after which she could make being with Matt her first priority.

On the field below, Matt glanced at the crowd as he headed for the visitors' dugout. CJ watched him disappear from sight and schooled her vision back to the field. Though it wasn't easy, CJ tried to blend in with the Los Angeles crowd. Trying not to cheer when Matt's team did well was almost as difficult as trying to watch the game instead of staring at her husband.

She held her breath when Matt stepped up to the plate for his first turn at bat. Connecting with the second pitch, he hit a line drive right at the shortstop who made the easy out. Like Matt, the other Phillies players struggled at the plate as the Dodgers' pitcher continued to throw strikes on the edge of the strike zone.

By the bottom of the eighth inning, Los Angeles led by five runs. Realizing that a loss for her husband's team was imminent, CJ picked up her purse and nudged Lacey, who stood and escorted her to the exit. Though CJ wanted to see the end of the game to support Matt, she felt it best to avoid the postgame traffic.

Numerous other fans apparently had the same idea. Already people were streaming from the stadium and heading for their cars. CJ hesitated when she and Lacey reached the crowded parking lot. Her tennis shoes crunched on the gravel, and the smell of exhaust assaulted her senses. Someone bumped into her and sent her stumbling forward, but Lacey grabbed her arm before she lost her balance completely.

As another large group of baseball fans swarmed past them, the image of hiding under the van in Minneapolis flashed in CJ's mind. She could remember too clearly the feel of the cold pavement beneath her, the sound of approaching footsteps. Why it appeared so vividly in her mind after almost two months, she didn't know. She could only guess that the stress from competing in three swim meets in as many days had left her both exhausted and vulnerable. Closing her eyes for a moment, she took a deep breath. When she opened her eyes, Lacey was still at her side, patiently waiting.

"Sorry," CJ muttered.

"Don't worry about it." He shook his head and took her by the arm. "Come on."

She let him lead her to the car, ignoring the pounding of her heart. She hated being afraid. For so long she had worked at convincing herself that she was living a normal life. Now that the day was quickly approaching that she would finally testify, she felt like she was starting over again.

After the trial, the government would no longer need her, their only obligation being to provide her with safety if she chose to remain in the Witness Protection Program. Until she saw Malloy at the swim meet in Minneapolis, she had decided to leave the program right after she testified. Now she wasn't so sure she would be able to.

While CJ looked on, Lacey went through his usual ritual of retrieving a tool from the trunk to examine the underside of the car. CJ's mood lightened when she considered the absurdity of the idea that someone had planted a bomb on a rental car in the middle of a crowded parking lot.

"You don't really think someone would plant a bomb with all of these people around, do you?" CJ asked, her voice carrying a touch of humor.

Lacey stopped just long enough to glance up at her. "No."

"Then why go through this exercise every time we go to a game?"

"Just standard operating procedure," Lacey said with a shrug. After checking beneath the car, he then popped the hood and completed his inspection. "If we really thought that going to Matt's games was a significant threat, we never would have let you anywhere near a stadium."

"I guess I never thought of it that way," CJ replied, her mood sobering once more as she considered how much research went into every little thing she did, from where she practiced to how she spent her free time.

Lacey opened the passenger side door for her and then rounded the hood and climbed into the driver's seat. "Are you and Matt still meeting at the beach after the game?"

CJ nodded.

"It's a bit of a drive. Let's head down there now and get some dinner." He started the car and put it in gear, glancing over at CJ. "Are you okay?"

"I'm sorry I panicked back there." CJ shook her head in frustration. "I just looked at all of those cars and felt like I couldn't breathe."

"You know, you're allowed to be human."

"I'll just be glad when all of this is over," CJ sighed. "It's hard to believe that after hiding for all of this time, the last trial is just a few weeks away."

Lacey studied her for a moment. "Do you really think that once Rush is behind bars you will feel safe?"

"I don't know. I just don't know if I can spend the rest of my life hiding." CJ turned to look out the window, barely noticing the palm trees scattered everywhere, from the landscaping outside of the stadium to the used car lot down the road.

Three hours later, CJ stepped out onto the beach alone. Over dinner she had reminded herself how lucky she was to have this time with Matt. Determined not to let her earlier panic attack ruin her date with her husband, CJ slipped her sandals off and stepped onto the cooling sand. She watched the waves crashing on the shore and lifted her face to the breeze coming off the water. A hodgepodge of people loitered on the beach and in the nearby clubs and bars, some still dressed in swimming suits and others dressed for the Los Angeles nightlife.

Lacey had settled down on the terrace of one of the restaurants overlooking the beach, looking very much like a local enjoying an after-dinner drink. Still, CJ felt safer knowing he was there.

The last of the sun's rays glistened off the Pacific Ocean just beyond the wide stretch of sand. Drawn to the nearly vacant beach, CJ started toward the water. She had only taken a few steps when she turned to see Matt approaching. He moved easily in the thinning crowd, his eyes scanning the scene until he saw her. As he closed the distance between them, his stride lengthened.

Their eyes locked and held, and everything else faded away. When she moved into his arms, CJ forgot the other people along the beach. There might have only been the two of them. She buried her head in his shoulder as his hand moved to her hair.

"Are you okay?" Matt ran a hand down her arm and back up again.

CJ nodded, emotions robbing her of her voice. She blinked back the tears that threatened and took a deep, cleansing breath before looking up at Matt. "I can't remember the last time we went out on a date together."

"Sure you can." Matt slipped an arm around her waist and started walking toward the water. "It was when you met me in Florida during spring training."

"I just wish I knew when I would see you next." CJ walked alongside him as darkness fell.

"It won't be much longer," Matt assured her. "One way or another, we'll work something out."

They walked in silence along the water's edge, the sound of the waves echoing over the cooling sand. Other couples walked past them hand in hand, but soon Matt and CJ found themselves alone on a stretch of beach not far from Lacey's watchful eye.

"What do you look forward to the most when all of this is over?" CJ asked, deliberately pushing Malloy from her mind.

"Seeing you sitting in the friends' box with all of the other players' wives."

"Really?" CJ stopped and turned to face him. "I thought visiting your family would be at the top of your list."

"They've been so good about visiting us that it hasn't really bothered me that much." Matt shrugged. "But every time we have a home game, I look into the friends' box and I hate that you aren't sitting there with the other wives."

"I never really thought about it before, but I'm sure it would be nice to sit with people who know what it's like to have their husbands gone half of the time."

"If I have my way, you will be coming with me on some of the road trips after you're done competing in the Olympics."

"Assuming I *make* the Olympics," CJ reminded him with a sigh. She brushed at some sand clinging to her capris, wishing she could brush away her doubts as easily. "Sometimes I wonder if it's all worth it. I spend so many hours training for a competition I may not even qualify for."

"You'll make it," Matt insisted.

CJ stopped, turning to face him. "Do you really think it's worth it?" Before he could answer, she pushed on, forcing herself to voice her doubts out loud. "Every time I compete, so many people risk their safety so that I can follow my dreams. If I come out of the Witness Protection Program, you could be at risk too."

"CJ, you're an athlete. This is what you do." Matt tugged on her hand so that she would fall into step beside him again. "Doug and the people protecting you understand that swimming is part of who you are and that it helps relieve the incredible amount of stress that comes from being a witness in a high-profile case."

"But how is that more important than the safety of the marshal that got shot in Minneapolis, or the agent that doubled for me here in LA?"

"If you hadn't been swimming, the government never would have known Malloy was even in the country," Matt pointed out. "Whether you realize it or not, your actions have helped the government as often as not."

"I don't know." She looked out at the waves crashing in over the sand. "Every night when I say my prayers, I wonder if this will be the night that I get the answer that it's time to stop swimming."

"And every night that answer doesn't come for a reason," Matt responded gently. "Besides, you can't give up on your dreams because you *might* not be fast enough. You would always regret not knowing."

"You're right." CJ nodded. "I just hope I don't have any more races like I did in Mission Viejo."

"Better there than at the Olympic trials. Besides, no one ever said it was going to be easy." Matt turned her into his arms, linking both hands around her waist.

"Are you trying to distract me?" CJ smiled when Matt brushed his lips across hers.

"Is it working?" Matt asked, running one hand up and then down her back.

"Mmmm." CJ closed her eyes and leaned into the kiss. The comfort and security she found in Matt's arms helped chase away the fears and doubts. Together they turned away from the water crashing behind them, both of them blissfully unaware of the man down the beach with a camera and a telephoto lens.

* * *

Matt looked down at his watch when the knock came at the hotel-room door. Seven o'clock in the morning. He was glad he had left his watch on East Coast time. Seven was early, but it sounded much better than four A.M. He opened the door and exchanged a tip for a room-service tray. He set the food on the table just as CJ came out of the bathroom.

They were going home today. Matt would leave first on a morning flight with the team, and CJ would leave a few hours later. Watching her break off a bite-size piece of muffin and pop it into her mouth, he wished their homes weren't over a thousand miles apart.

"Do you want some?" CJ asked, offering him half of the muffin.

Matt shook his head as the phone rang. He snatched it up on the second ring. "Hello?"

Katherine Whitmore's voice came over the phone. "Matt, we have to talk."

"Hi, Mom." Reconsidering his wife's offer, Matt reached over and broke off a piece of her muffin. "What's up?"

"Have you seen the newspaper today?"

"Which one?" Matt wondered, grinning as he snatched the last of CJ's breakfast.

"Any of them." Concern coated Katherine's normally calm voice. "Matt, the pictures are everywhere. The tabloids, the newspapers, the Internet . . ."

"Pictures?" Matt interrupted, wondering if his father's latest political stand on the homeless had landed him on the wrong side of the press. "Pictures of what?"

"Pictures of you." Katherine hesitated, choosing her words carefully. "You on the beach, at your hotel."

"What?" Matt interrupted, standing abruptly. The chair he had been sitting on crashed to the floor as he pushed away from the table and began to pace. If CJ had been photographed with him . . . He couldn't even finish the thought. Still he forced himself to ask the question. "Are you telling me that I'm not alone in these pictures?"

"I'm sorry, Matt, but that's exactly what I'm telling you," Katherine said. "One of your father's aides came across one in the *Washington Post,* and I'm afraid his research turned up several others."

"I'll call you back later," Matt sighed. "Thanks."

"What's wrong?" CJ asked as soon as Matt hung up the phone.

"Call Doug." Matt retrieved CJ's cell phone from her purse and handed it to her.

"Why?"

"My mom said there are pictures of us in the paper this morning." Matt picked up the hotel phone again and pressed the button for the concierge.

"Oh, no," CJ breathed, the color draining from her face. She flipped open her phone and pressed speed dial for Doug. While she quickly told Doug about Matt's phone call, Matt asked the concierge to send up a copy of every newspaper they carried.

As soon as CJ hung up, Matt asked, "What did Doug say?"

"He's on his way up." CJ moved into his arms and looked up at him, tears threatening.

"Don't worry." Matt brushed her hair back from her face and tried to think of something positive. "At least this didn't happen a couple of days ago."

The first tear spilled over, and CJ voiced the worst of her fears. "What if Doug says we can't be together, that Malloy will keep coming after me? How can we spend the rest of our lives trying to steal bits of time together? That's not a real life."

"CJ, it can't be that bad," Matt said, hoping his words were true. "Worst case, I come up with some kind of injury and quit baseball so we can go hide out in some little town where no one has ever heard of us. I can be a sheepherder or farmer or something."

"Stop trying to cheer me up." CJ's lips curled up at the thought of her husband trying to herd a bunch of sheep. "This is serious."

"And we'll deal with it," Matt assured her. "I mean, how bad can it be?"

Ten minutes later CJ, Matt, and Doug stared at the stack of newspapers the bellboy had delivered a few moments earlier. "This is bad."

The photographs and articles featuring CJ and Matt appeared in all the local newspapers, as well as in some tabloids. A large photograph, undoubtedly taken their first night in town, graced the front page of one tabloid. Matt was standing on the balcony, CJ swept up in his embrace, both laughing and both easily identifiable. Ironically, the only people that would recognize CJ as Matt's wife were his family and the men trying to kill her. A smaller photograph showed CJ and Matt kissing on the beach, leaving no doubt as to the romantic nature of their relationship.

Other papers contained smaller articles, some in the society pages and others in the sports section. Each one featured clear images of Matt and CJ together.

Matt dropped into a chair as reality set in. They were going to find her. Rush's trial was just weeks away, and Matt's fame might very well cost him the one thing he held most dear.

He felt CJ's hand on his shoulder as she perused the articles in front of them. He couldn't even look at her. How could he ever forgive himself if something happened to her? He knew it wasn't his fault that the photographs existed, but he hadn't become a professional baseball player by accident.

CJ stood for a moment by his side, her hand caressing his arm as she stared at the front page of a trashy magazine. "Matt, you have to let the Secret Service assign someone to protect you."

"I'm not worried about me," Matt said pointedly.

"I am." CJ's voice cracked, and she took a deep breath before continuing. "I can hide out. You can't hide without giving up your career."

"I'm not in any danger. Hurting me serves no purpose." Matt forced himself to look at his wife.

"She's right," Doug interrupted. "You need to have some protection, if for no other reason than to give CJ some comfort."

"I don't see any point . . ." Matt trailed off when he caught the expression on Doug's face. He was right. CJ wasn't going to be able to function if she spent all of her time worrying about him. "Okay, I'll have Dad send a couple of Secret Service agents my way until after Rush's trial."

"Thank you." CJ leaned down and kissed his cheek. She began flipping through the tabloid on the top of the stack. "I don't think this looks too much like me."

"Yeah, it does." Matt looked at the next paper in the stack, the *Washington Post*. He flipped through several sections before finding the photographs on the third page of the Style section.

"Doug, why don't you sit down?" CJ motioned to a chair. "You two can find the articles, and I'll cut them out."

"Why are you cutting them out?" Matt asked, wondering briefly if CJ was losing her mind.

"Someday, we're all going to look back on this day and laugh about this." CJ lifted her eyes to meet his, worry showing despite her light words. "We might as well save the evidence of how bad it really was."

Matt's eyes looked on CJ's. "Do you understand that Rush is going to know that we're still together? He's going to send someone after you again."

"He's going to send someone after me no matter what we do." CJ's voice took on an edge. "We knew it was going to get worse before it got better. We just didn't know it was going to get this bad." She glanced briefly at Doug before continuing. "Come on. Someday, our kids are going to want to see these."

Matt stared at her for a moment, cheered slightly by her mention of the future they had planned. It wouldn't help to think of all of the obstacles they still had to overcome. Instead, he pushed thoughts of challenges aside, determined to believe that they could still create a life together.

He stared down at the grainy photographs again, studying them more closely. *He* could definitely tell that it was CJ in the photos with him, but would everyone else be able to identify her? Her hair was lighter since she moved to Florida, and the length had changed over the years from long to boyishly short to its current medium length.

"You should cut your hair," Matt declared, finally setting down the newspaper he held.

"I was thinking the same thing." CJ set one of the clipped articles aside. "Of course, I'll have to adjust all of my goggles again."

Matt had to smile. Here she was facing another assassination attempt, and she was worried about her goggles. "You still have a few weeks until the trials."

He settled down at the table, hoping that the future they were speaking of was only a few weeks away.

CHAPTER 20

Jimmy Malloy tugged at the sleeve of his suit jacket and tried to ignore the sweltering heat. He rapped a knuckle against the door of the apartment that was the last-known address of Christal Jones, a.k.a. Kylie Ramsey.

A tall blond answered the door and gave him a questioning look. Malloy mentally flipped through his research and identified her as Jill Lancaster, one of Christal Jones's previous roommates.

Malloy offered her a business card that claimed he was a reporter for the *Dallas Morning News.* "I am doing a story on Kylie Ramsey, and I hoped I could ask you a few questions."

Jill glanced at her watch before answering. "I was actually just on my way out. I'm afraid I have a meeting in a few minutes."

"Oh." Malloy let a little disappointment lace his voice. "Well, would you be able to direct me to any of her other friends here in town? I really wanted to get some behind-the-scenes kind of information before she competes in the Olympic trials."

"She made the Olympic trials?" Jill asked, surprised. "I had no idea."

"That's why I've been assigned to do a story on her."

"Well, you might ask around at the college, but she didn't socialize a lot while she lived here." Jill picked up her purse from the table by the door and stepped outside, closing the door behind her.

Malloy stepped back and nodded, trying not to look annoyed. "I'll try that."

Jill stepped toward the parking lot. "Good luck."

"Thanks." Malloy waited for her to take a few steps. "Oh, one last thing. I wonder if you might know if she has a good-luck charm—you know, something she always carries with her."

Jill gave him an odd look. "Not that I know of. Sorry I couldn't be more help."

Malloy watched her climb into her car. As she put the car in gear and drove past him, she gave a smile and a wave. He took several steps toward the car he had rented, then stopped as soon as Jill's car pulled out of sight. Glancing quickly around the parking lot, he reversed course and walked back to Jill's front door.

With one last look around, he retrieved a case from the inside pocket of his jacket, quickly selecting a tool. He inserted it into the lock, working it for nearly fifteen seconds before the lock clicked open. Using a handkerchief, he opened the door, and without a backwards glance, he stepped into the apartment and closed the door behind him.

He stood motionless just inside the door for a full minute, listening for any life within the apartment. His research told him that Jill lived by herself, but surprises had been known to happen. Removing a pair of gloves from his pocket, he pulled them on, grateful that he appeared to be alone.

Making a quick sweep of the apartment, he took in the Southwestern décor and photographs hanging on the walls. One bedroom was completely empty, and a second had been fashioned into a den. The third bedroom obviously belonged to Jill.

Malloy began in this bedroom, searching quickly for diaries, photographs, or anything that might reveal information about the former roommate or the diamonds she most certainly had in her possession. A shoebox filled with photographs revealed nothing, as did the framed photos hanging on the walls. In fact, he was unable to find a single photo with Christal Jones in it.

Working rapidly, he checked the den and the empty bedroom, and then moved on to the living room. Frustrated at his lack of success, he started yanking open kitchen drawers. A search of the junk drawer finally proved he was in the right place, as he discovered a photograph of Jill, Christal Jones, and another girl. He assumed the third girl to be the roommate who had recently moved out.

The photograph had clearly been taken inside the apartment, the three of them sitting on the couch, their arms slung casually around each other. Christal sat on the left, one arm around Jill, and in the other hand she held a small teddy bear. Malloy studied it for a long moment. The men he had sent after the cop had mentioned that the girl was holding a stuffed animal when she had gone into the bedroom. He shook his head, wondering if it could really be that easy. Was the teddy bear the hiding place? Could she really have been carrying around millions of dollars worth of diamonds and never realized what she had?

Malloy slipped the photo into his jacket pocket and quickly made sure that the apartment looked just as it had when he arrived. Then, with a rare smile on his face, Malloy let himself out and strolled over to his rental car. If all went well, he expected those diamonds would be in his hands very shortly.

* * *

Jill waited by the front door while Doug went through her apartment. He had planned his flight back from LA to go through Dallas so they could spend some time together, but this wasn't exactly what she'd had in mind. A minute passed before he motioned her inside and closed the door.

"Look around," Doug said in his official voice. "See if anything looks out of place."

Still rooted just inside, Jill set her purse on the table by the door and glanced around the living room. "Everything looks exactly the same," she sighed, embarrassed that her description of her unexpected visitor had landed them at her apartment instead of at the Dallas restaurant where they had planned to eat. "I'm sorry, Doug. I must have overreacted. That guy just really gave me the creeps, and he was asking such weird questions."

"I don't think you overreacted," Doug replied. "Look around and see if anything is missing."

Reluctantly, Jill went to her room and checked her jewelry box, finding that the pearl necklace her mother had given her was still inside. She checked the drawer where she kept some emergency cash hidden and found it undisturbed. After glancing in the other bedrooms, she went into the kitchen, where Doug was dusting for fingerprints.

"What are you doing?" Jill asked, watching him swirl the little brush over her cabinets and drawers. "It doesn't look like anyone was in here. I haven't found anything missing."

"Has anyone been in the apartment besides you in the last day or two?"

Jill shook her head. "Why?"

"I smelled a trace of men's cologne when I first walked in. Someone has been in here today." Doug stood up and shook his head. "I'll have to run these prints through the lab, but I have a feeling they all belong to you and me. If it doesn't look like anything was disturbed, this guy must be a professional."

"A professional what?" Jill's eyes widened.

"Criminal." Doug crossed to her and put his hands on her arms. "Come on. Let's get you packed. You aren't staying here anymore."

"What?" Jill looked at him, stunned.

"This guy was looking for CJ. I'm not going to stand by and watch you get caught in the crossfire."

"I don't believe this." Jill shook her head. "What am I going to do with my stuff? Our house isn't ready yet."

"Pack up what you want to keep with you for now." Doug pulled out his cell phone. "I'll have everything else moved into storage until we can move into the house."

"Where am I supposed to stay?"

"Between my family and yours, I'm sure we can work something out." Doug nodded toward her bedroom. "Go ahead and pack. I'll take care of everything else."

Jill took a few steps before turning back to Doug. "Is this what it's like for CJ?"

Doug evaded the question. "It'll be over soon."

* * *

They were everywhere. Matt stared at the hordes of paparazzi outside of his building, cameras perched in readiness. The phone call from his parents had warned him that something like this might happen, but he hadn't anticipated anything on this scale.

After growing up in the political spotlight, dealing with reporters was second nature to Matt. However, the reporters that had occasionally snapped his picture throughout his teenage and early college years seemed minor compared to the swarm blocking the entrance to his building. With the senator's help, Doug had assigned Matt two Secret Service agents for his safety. Matt was beginning to wonder if they were supposed to protect him from the people in Rush's organization or from the media circus unfolding downstairs.

Though he still believed that Rush and those working for him would be wasting their time coming after him, the possibility existed. For all he knew, Rush had men disguised as reporters waiting for him downstairs. Since Rush's trial was already underway, he was much more worried about his wife's safety. From what he had been told, the prosecution would use CJ as their final witness, thus laying the groundwork for her testimony.

Knowing how many times Rush had tried and failed to silence CJ, Matt was grateful for the security of the Secret Service. If nothing else, he hoped they would be able to spot anyone trying to locate CJ through him.

Matt waited in his condo until one of the Secret Service agents came to get him after clearing a path to the parking garage beneath the building. He wasn't sure how they managed to get him out of his condo, into the government vehicle, and to the stadium unnoticed.

The press had taken every opportunity to hound Matt at the game the day before. For security reasons, management had limited the number of reporters in the clubhouse that night. Matt was surprised the team had even extended that assistance after he had refused to give any kind of statement to them or the press.

Matt breathed a sigh of relief when he made it into the locker room and only had to deal with the questioning looks of his teammates. They all knew he was a Latter-day Saint, and over the past season, many of them had come to understand his moral standards. With the pictures of him and CJ at his hotel room and the suggestive headlines and stories in the tabloids, he worried that everyone thought that he had let down his standards—the same standards that many thought were set too high to begin with.

Tensions were already rising as talk of a trade continued. Everyone knew that someone on the team was about to be traded, and rumors had leaked out that Matt wanted to be that someone. Naturally, his teammates wondered why he didn't want to stay with them.

Now that Matt and CJ had been linked together in the papers, he wasn't sure a trade was in his future after all. As he looked around the locker room, though, he knew that staying wasn't going to be any easier than going.

Shortly after the team completed batting practice, the team manager called Matt into his office. Matt took the seat across from him, not sure what to expect.

"Well, kid, it looks like you aren't going to be with the Phillies after tonight." The manager handed Matt a file which outlined the details of his trade to the Florida Marlins.

Matt stared at the file. For weeks he had hoped and prayed this would happen, but he hadn't known how complicated his life would become when those prayers were answered. If he had been traded just a week earlier, he never would have met CJ in California and they wouldn't have been photographed together. Now if he moved to Florida, he could be leading Rush's men right to CJ. Of course, he had no choice now; the negotiations were already finished.

Still stunned by the news, Matt managed to exchange pleasantries with the manager before heading off to call Keith. He wondered if Keith knew that the arrangements had been finalized, or if this would be a shock to him too.

CHAPTER 21

Keith sat at Matt's kitchen table examining the agreement with the Florida Marlins. For several reasons, he had been given the assignment to negotiate Matt's contract. Like many other agents in the FBI, he held a law degree. In addition, he was one of a select few that knew CJ's current location.

Biting into a piece of the pizza that Matt had ordered, Keith read through the last page of the contract. The deal was perfect, or as close to perfect as Keith thought he could manage, especially since he hadn't worked with this type of contract in several years. The five-year agreement gave Matt job security, relocated him to Miami, and would earn him a generous salary.

"What are we going to do?" Matt asked, breaking into Keith's thoughts. "How can I move to Miami if CJ is there?"

"It isn't as bad as it seems," Keith replied. "Several teams were interested in trading for you. I basically just set up your demands to suit the Marlins and discourage other teams from pursuing you."

"What do you mean?" Matt fiddled with the cap on his water bottle.

"Florida was burned a couple of times last year when contracts came up for renewal and players they wanted to keep either chose to go elsewhere or demanded so much money they couldn't afford to keep them. Because of that, I guessed that they would jump at a five-year deal, especially since you can play more than one position." Keith shrugged. "I knew that most teams wouldn't go for a longer-term contract since you haven't been in the league that long."

"I still don't understand how this helps us."

"Because we didn't go out and approach only Florida, no one should suspect that this is exactly where you wanted to go," Keith explained. "If Malloy or Rush has anyone watching you, they are more likely to look for CJ in California where you were seen with her, or here in Philadelphia."

"I hope you're right," Matt said, exhaling slowly.

"Either way, I set you up in an apartment in Broward County to start with. The FBI and the Marshals will reevaluate our security plans for CJ as soon as Rush's trial is over. At that point, we'll see what arrangements can be made for you and CJ."

"I just wish you could find Malloy."

"Don't we all."

* * *

As CJ approached the pool, she ran her fingers through her chin-length hair. While the publicity about Matt and her had been bad in Los Angeles, the articles had mostly been limited to the LA papers. The main threat to CJ in Miami was the tabloids that popped up on occasion and the photos floating around on the Internet. In case someone in Miami did take notice of the trashy photos, CJ had gotten a haircut, and she expected that her new look would keep anyone from recognizing her as the woman with Matt Whitmore. At the insistence of Tara and Lacey, CJ had severely limited her appearances in public, so she doubted it would matter anyway.

Pete walked toward her, his coaching briefcase slung over his shoulder. "Well, I have some good news and some bad news."

"I've already had enough bad news for the year," CJ informed him. "Why don't you just tell me about the good news and we'll forget about the bad news for today."

Ignoring her, Pete pulled a file out of his bag. "I looked up the results from all of the meets for last weekend. Looking at your competition worldwide, you have a decent shot at a medal in the 200 breaststroke."

"I assume that's the good news."

Pete shrugged. "Unfortunately, the best woman in the event is also American."

"Bridget Bannon," CJ stated with resignation in her voice. "What about the 200 IM?"

"The competition is tighter for you there. Getting to the finals will be a challenge, but if you can make it there, you have a shot. The good news is that I have you as the top 100 breaststroker in the States, which means you should be able to claim the medley relay spot."

"If I can qualify," CJ sighed.

"I think I've worked that one out." Pete handed her a meet application sheet. "This meet is in North Carolina in two weeks."

"That's only a few days before I have to testify at Rush's trial," CJ explained. "Isn't there a meet a week or two later? Maybe then I wouldn't be such a target."

"This is the best choice." Pete handed her a meet schedule. "All the other possible meets you could use are in LA, Baltimore, or Europe."

CJ's eyes brightened at the mention of Europe.

Before she could say anything, Pete cut her off. "No, we are not going to Europe."

"Oh, come on Pete." CJ pointed at the schedule. "There's one here that's a week after I testify. It's perfect."

"Nice try, kiddo." Pete shook his head. "You would lose too much practice time, and your body wouldn't have enough time to adjust to the time change before you would compete."

"I assume LA is out because of the media attention," CJ guessed.

Pete nodded. "And Baltimore is out because your old team will be there."

"Then I guess we're going to North Carolina."

* * *

Doug Valdez stared at the television monitor in front of him, wondering how long he had been sitting in the airport security office. He still couldn't believe the news Toblin had given him just that morning. Malloy's last confirmed location was Miami.

Though his first instinct had been to pull CJ from the house in Coral Gables and relocate her to the Midwest somewhere, he reconsidered when he realized that she was probably safer staying where she was. Any move this close to the trial would require bringing in extra personnel, and Doug wasn't about to let anyone new near CJ.

The security tapes from the Miami airport were logged by date, time, and location. Already Doug had watched countless hours of the tapes, trying to find out when Malloy had left the airport and where he had gone. He knew there had to be something on these tapes that would help him find the man that had been eluding him for the past three years.

"I don't see him near any of the exits," Doug told the security chief for the airport. "Let's go back to where he exited the plane and see if we can track his movements that way."

The man nodded, retrieving two tapes. "This one would pick him up if he headed for baggage claim, and that one goes the other direction."

"Let's see what we can find." Doug settled back in his seat as the first tape was loaded.

Four hours later, Doug finally found his answer. Malloy had gone to baggage claim only to blend in with the other passengers. He must have tucked himself into a blind spot, because the cameras didn't pick him up for over an hour when he finally left the baggage claim area. He was then sighted moving toward a ticket counter.

Through painstaking work, Doug came to realize that Malloy wasn't in Miami after all. Rather, he had just been there for a very long layover. The camera that picked him up in the gate area only had a partial view of the waiting area. Only one airline flew out of the three gates he could have accessed, and with some help from the airline personnel, Doug was able to narrow down the possibilities.

Of the three gates, only two had flights leaving around the time that Malloy finally disappeared from their sight for good. One went to the Cayman Islands, and the other went to Curacao. The airlines informed him that the flight to Grand Cayman had not offered any connections that particular night. However, the flight to Curacao had two connections that left before the airport closed that night. One was to Bonaire, and the other was to Aruba.

Though his work day should have ended hours earlier, Doug went back to his office and pulled out a number for Interpol. If he could give them the dates and times, he hoped they could use the same method of scanning surveillance tapes to help him locate Malloy.

* * *

"I can't believe Doug is really going to let me try again." CJ shifted in the backseat of the rental car and watched Pete look over the meet information. They had flown into

Charlotte the night before from the Southwest Florida Airport. CJ didn't know why Doug wouldn't let them fly out of Miami, but after he had relocated her to such an incredible house, she doubted he could do much at this point to surprise her.

"I can be persuasive when I want to be," Pete told her, not looking up. "Besides, you're only going to be at the meet for about two minutes."

"Excuse me?"

Before Pete could respond, Tara looked back at them. "We're here."

CJ looked up to see that Lacey had pulled into the parking lot of a country club. "What are we doing here?"

"Warming up," Pete told her. "The FBI has an agent doubling for you at the meet. She will help us time it right so that you get to the meet just in time to walk in, step up on the blocks, swim the breaststroke, preferably in under a minute ten, and get back in the car. Then we'll come back here so you can cool down."

"You were serious." CJ shook her head in amazement. "I really will be there for about two minutes."

"That's the plan." Pete pointed at a gate on the side of the clubhouse. "Now let's get going. We have a timetable to keep."

The timing was perfect. CJ finished her warm-up with five minutes to spare, and they had already arrived in the parking lot when the signal came that her heat was coming up. Pete went into the meet first and claimed a spot on deck while CJ prepared for her race. When the heat before hers started, Lacey and Tara escorted her to the block.

CJ positioned her goggles, stepped up on the blocks, and an instant later was in the water swimming her favorite event. She started out in front and stayed there, each stroke giving her a little more distance from the other swimmers.

When she hit the timing pad, she looked up at the scoreboard and stared. Next to her name it read 1:08.06. She had
qualified with over four seconds to spare.

Tara didn't give her time to revel in her success, instead
handing her a towel as she climbed out of the pool and then
guiding her out to the parking lot. As soon as CJ was in the
car, Lacey drove the car away.

"What about Pete?" CJ asked, surprised they were leaving
him behind.

"He needs to get your proof of time. We have a car waiting
for him, and he'll meet us back at the hotel," Tara said.

They went back to the country club, where CJ took her
time in the water. When she finished cooling down, they
drove to the hotel. She was just unlocking the door to her
room when Tara's phone rang.

The conversation was brief, lasting only long enough for
CJ to walk into her room and drop her things on the bed, but
as soon as Tara hung up she turned to CJ. "I don't have time
to explain but we only have five minutes to change and pack."

Before CJ could ask why, Tara left the room. Worried
that something was wrong, CJ changed her clothes and
stuffed her wet towel and swimsuit into a bag.

No explanations were offered as she was rushed off to the
train station, and she quickly realized that Tara and Lacey
didn't know much more than she did. Once on the train,
Lacey led her and Tara to a sleeping compartment. He and
Tara checked it out, as well as the adjoining compartment
where Lacey and Pete would stay the night. As soon as they
were satisfied, Lacey motioned CJ inside.

"Why don't you two wait here, and Pete and I'll go get us
some dinner?" Lacey suggested.

"That would be great," CJ agreed, sitting down on what
would be her bed that night. "I'm starving."

Tara pulled the door closed and sat across from her. "I hope they remember dessert."

"Don't count on it if Pete chooses the menu." CJ felt the train start forward. "Now that we're moving, are you going to tell me what's going on?"

"I'm still not sure," Tara admitted. "I just know that there was a security breach at the airport, and Doug wanted you out of town just in case it was someone looking for you."

"What kind of security breach?"

"I don't know. Today we're just following orders." Tara leaned back. "I have to admit, I'm glad that you're done with swim meets for a while. This is just way too stressful."

"You're telling me," CJ agreed, thinking of the Olympic trials that were only four weeks away.

CHAPTER 22

This was the day—the day CJ had both looked forward to and dreaded for so long. Tara stood by the hotel room window, watching the movement on the street below. Outside the door, two more U.S. Marshals stood guard. Rush's trial had started nearly three weeks earlier, and CJ would be the final witness for the prosecution.

Suddenly, Tara turned from the window. "Let's move."

CJ moved toward the door, quickly surrounded by those determined to protect her. They rode the elevator to the underground parking garage and then climbed into an unmarked car. To her left, CJ could see a similar car pulling out of the parking garage, flanked by two police cars.

As though reading her thoughts, Tara nodded to the other vehicles. "If someone tries for you, hopefully they'll go for the decoy."

CJ took a deep breath, praying that Rush's men wouldn't succeed in hurting her or anyone else. Already he had destroyed so many lives, and CJ knew his men would not hesitate to kill in order to further his evil designs. The marshals and CJ waited in the parking lot until the marshals received the signal that it was safe to leave. Fifteen minutes later, they entered the courthouse.

Nerves fluttered in CJ's stomach as she was led into the courtroom. The heels of her shoes clicked on the tile floor as the young bailiff led her to the stand. Even though CJ tried to school her eyes away from Rush, she couldn't help looking over to the defense's side of the courtroom.

She remembered the first time she had met this man. Matt had introduced her to Judge Chris Rush at a brunch his parents had hosted. Rush and his wife had chatted companionably with her and Matt, and everything in the judge's behavior had suggested that he was the good friend Matt's parents believed him to be.

Looking at him now, CJ wondered if she would ever be able to forget his face and what he had put her through. The former judge had changed significantly, his polished persona and air of wealth and stature apparently worn away by his time spent in prison. Yet, despite the gray hair and pallor of his skin, CJ remembered well what the man in front of her was capable of.

For three years, Rush had sat in prison awaiting trial for an assortment of crimes including conspiracy, murder, and smuggling. Shortly after he was arrested, bail had been denied because he had tried to flee the country and had the means to attempt to do so again. Rush had then used the legal system to his advantage by delaying his own trial in an effort to allow his stooges to eliminate the witnesses against him. Originally the government had expected CJ to testify within twelve to eighteen months after Rush's arrest, rather than three years.

Rush looked up and returned CJ's stare, and she shuddered. He didn't look like an evil man, but she knew better. The organization he headed had been nothing short of ruthless. Anyone who threatened its success was eliminated. Standard operating policy.

Three years ago, Chase had been the greatest threat Rush's organization had ever faced. The knowledge he had gained working undercover had cost him his life. His few dying words had given CJ the pieces to the puzzle to ultimately identify Rush as the criminal he truly was. Chase had been her dearest friend, and she owed it to him to make his efforts pay off.

CJ swallowed hard, barely hearing the words as she was sworn in until the final phrase, "so help you God." She took a deep breath, saying a silent prayer as she took her seat. The bailiff that had escorted her now stood a few feet away on the side of the courtroom. Another bailiff, slightly older and rounder, stood in front of the double doors that led to the hallway. The judge had apparently seen the wisdom in ordering a closed courtroom, and the only people in the spectator seats were two federal marshals. In front of them were the prosecuting attorneys on one side, and Rush and his defense team on the other.

CJ answered the prosecutor's questions easily, as she was well rehearsed from testifying in previous trials. The proceedings rested for lunch before the defense was permitted to begin their cross-examination. CJ answered the defense attorney's first few questions easily enough, but when he began asking her about Chase's final words, her throat closed up as she tried to fight back her emotions.

"Miss Jones, you testified earlier that Chase's final words were 'Chris Rush. Don't let him find you.' Is that correct?"

"Yes." CJ nodded.

"Did Chase ever call you by the name Chris?"

CJ struggled not to let memories of Chase's death overwhelm her. "Sometimes."

"Isn't it possible that he was simply calling you by name, telling you to hurry and hide?"

"That is what I thought at first, but . . ."

"Just answer the question," the attorney snapped.

"At one time, I did believe that was his meaning," CJ replied, fighting to keep her voice even. She knew that the prosecutors would have a chance to redirect, and she looked forward to clarifying that she had also seen Christopher Rush's name on the organizational chart at Chase's apartment.

Throughout the afternoon, the defense attorneys continued to try to distort CJ's testimony. They were good, but even with their attempts to discredit CJ, they were unable to damage her credibility or cover up the truth through their cross-examination.

Finally, after several hours of testimony, cross-examination, and redirect, CJ was escorted out of the courtroom by two U.S. Marshals.

Security was tighter than CJ had ever seen it, a wall of federal officers waiting for her just outside the courtroom. They moved to shield her as they led her through the hallway, down the stairs, and out a side door. The air was thick with humidity as they stepped out into the late-afternoon heat. In the distance, CJ could see the Washington Monument against the gray sky.

She slid into the waiting car and looked around nervously. Was that really it? Except for being face-to-face with Rush, the trial had not been much different from the others she had testified in. Somehow she had thought she would feel a great sense of relief and freedom when it was over, but she felt neither. Of course, the possibility still remained that Rush could be acquitted, but she wasn't going to think about that. Certainly after the overwhelming evidence the prosecution had presented, the jurors would see the truth, and the evidence would hold up to the standard "beyond a reasonable doubt."

Glancing outside, CJ watched pedestrians along the sidewalks. Her nerves buzzed as she remembered what it was like to walk outside without the protection of the government.

As though reading her mind, Tara spoke. "Are you ready to be rid of us?"

"I can't even remember what it's like to not have you guys around."

"Well, we'll still be around at least through the Olympic trials, and probably through the Olympics." Tara checked the vehicles on her side of the car as they started their circuitous route back to the hotel. Without looking over at CJ, Tara added, "I am counting on a free trip to the Olympics, so you had better not let me down."

"I'll do what I can," CJ said wryly. She glanced back as the courthouse disappeared from view. "How much longer do you think the trial will last?"

"It's hard to say. A week, maybe two."

"I hope it's over soon."

"I know."

* * *

Doug tapped his pen anxiously on the pad of paper in front of him. He had been waiting for this call from Interpol for weeks.

"We think Malloy's hiding out in Bonaire," the Interpol agent informed him.

"How long do you think it will take to track him down?" Doug asked, afraid to get his hopes up.

"That's hard to say. We already have the airport staked out, and the island authorities have a couple of boats strategically placed to check out anyone who is island hopping or heading for Venezuela. The island only has about ten thousand residents, so he won't be able to hide for long, especially since we now have the entrance visas from the day Malloy arrived. We'll check out all of the addresses for those that entered that day. Eventually we'll find him."

"The sooner the better," Doug declared, wishing there was something more he could do to move things along.

"I'll check in with you in a couple of days unless something develops sooner."

"I appreciate it." Doug hung up the phone. Now that CJ had finished testifying, Malloy was the last credible threat to her. Doug didn't know if Malloy was operating under Rush's orders or if Malloy was worried that someday CJ might testify against him. Regardless, the Olympic trials were going to be a logistical nightmare if Malloy was still at large by then.

Logically, Doug knew that he should try to prevent CJ from swimming in the Olympic trials if Malloy was still out there. Emotionally, however, Doug worried that if he pushed the issue, CJ would simply choose to leave protective custody. She might just be willing to take the chance once Rush was convicted, especially since she was so anxious to be with Matt again.

Matt had already moved to Florida, or more accurately, his belongings had been relocated to Florida. He had joined up with the Marlins in time to play just two home games before they had left on a long road trip. Doug hoped that by the time Matt returned the next evening, the final verdict for Rush's trial would be in. Maybe then they could all relax a little.

* * *

Jimmy Malloy took one last look around his house by the ocean. He hated to lose it, but sometimes one had to sacrifice the things one held most dear. Malloy glanced over at Miguel lying on the couch. The drugs Malloy had put into Miguel's drink earlier that evening had taken full effect and would not wear off until it was too late. Miguel had been a loyal employee for nearly three years. Malloy regretted that their friendship had to end this way, but what else could he do? The police needed to find a body or his plan wouldn't work.

He knew the cops might order an autopsy, but Malloy had already taken care of that potential problem. He had paid off a local dentist so that the dental records used for identification would reveal that Jimmy Malloy had died in the fire, rather than Miguel Artez. It was amazing what some people would do for money.

Picking up Miguel's passport and the last of his things, Malloy placed his own wallet and passport into Miguel's jacket pocket. He then picked up the book of matches from the coffee table. Striking one, he let it fall into the wooden bin filled with discarded newspapers. The flames grew immediately, rapidly eating through the paper and then flickering as the wood caught on fire.

Jimmy moved toward the front door, looking back at the fire as it licked at the curtains. With one last look around, he walked out of the house and got into Miguel's car. He started down the hill, checking his watch. He stopped as he left the neighborhood, looking out over the ocean. Ten minutes later, he could see the smoke pluming from his home. Malloy started once again toward the airport, refusing to look back.

He knew that Interpol had people at the airport, but he doubted they would remain for long once they determined that he was dead. Relying on his patience, Malloy stopped at a restaurant and forced himself to linger over lunch. After finishing his meal, he browsed the souvenir shops and bought himself a few Bonaire T-shirts and two pairs of incredibly boring khaki shorts. He took his new clothes and finally headed for the hotel where he had checked in the day before.

Airport security would be high for the next day or so until dental records confirmed that Jimmy Malloy—not Miguel Artez—had died in the mysterious fire. Malloy knew he could afford to wait for a while longer.

CHAPTER 23

Doug stared at the report for a full five minutes before reality sank in. Malloy was dead. Interpol was still waiting on the full autopsy report, but the dental records had matched. After years of running from the FBI and other agencies, Malloy had been killed by a competing drug lord. At least that was the theory. No one in Interpol seemed to be buying the possibility that it was an accidental fire, and so far their investigation suggested that one of Malloy's competitors would have the most to gain from his death.

How he was killed didn't really matter to Doug. He was just relieved that this case was nearly closed. In a matter of hours or days, Rush would be found guilty, and CJ and Matt could finally get on with their lives. The DNA testing that would complete the identification of Jimmy Malloy would take a few more weeks, but the initial findings appeared pretty solid. Remnants of Malloy's credit cards had even been found on the body.

Doug's first instinct was to call CJ and tell her the good news, but instead he pushed aside another file he had been working on and began outlining security options. Now that Malloy was no longer a threat, things would need to be adjusted. Doug was just getting ready to walk out the office door on Monday evening when he got the call he had been waiting for. The verdict was in.

* * *

Tuesday morning CJ pulled two bags of groceries out of the trunk and followed Lacey into the house. She was a bit surprised that he had let her go grocery shopping with him after her early-morning practice. She hoped it was a sign of confidence that Rush would be found guilty. Though she was trying not to think about it, the verdict was always in the back of her mind. She only took two steps into the kitchen before she stopped cold.

Several moving boxes were stacked on the kitchen counters, and Pete and another man were in the backyard working on the security system. Tara walked into the kitchen carrying yet another box. She took one look at Lacey and glared. "Next time, I get to go with CJ and you can do all of the lifting."

CJ spoke before Lacey could respond. "What's going on?"

Tara set down the box, opened it, and pulled out CJ's wheat grinder. "What's going on is I need to know where you want to put all of your stuff."

"What?" CJ looked from Tara to Lacey, unable to fathom why the government would move her things to a safehouse. When Doug walked around the corner, CJ's chest tightened. Could the verdict have come back "not guilty"? Was this to become her permanent hiding place? Her future with Matt, her dreams for the Olympics . . . CJ couldn't even finish the thought.

"Did you tell her?" Doug asked, moving to give CJ a hug.

CJ braced for the news. "Tell me what?"

"The verdict is in." Doug grinned down at her, his arm still draped loosely around her shoulders. "He's guilty."

CJ sighed heavily, tears springing into her eyes. She took a deep breath and then another before she looked around once more. "If he's guilty, why is my stuff here? And why are they working on the security system?"

"Matt and I both thought that we should upgrade the system with more visual capabilities since you won't have the marshals living with you anymore."

"When did you talk to Matt?"

Just then Matt entered from the hallway. He grinned at CJ, his eyes full of mischief as he spoke. "Doug, you can let go of my wife now."

"Matt!" CJ rushed forward and jumped into his arms. She held on tight for a moment before thinking to ask the most obvious question. "What are you doing here?"

"I live here." Matt grinned. "You're right. It is a great house."

"I don't understand." CJ looked from Matt to Doug.

"Matt bought this house from the government this morning," Doug informed her. "I guess the Marlins are paying him pretty well."

Warily, CJ asked, "But what about Malloy?"

"He's dead. The coroner in Bonaire tentatively confirmed that yesterday, saying that Malloy's dental records matched the teeth of the deceased. However, because the death was suspicious, they're doing some DNA testing, and it will be a few weeks before we get the final confirmation. But it looks like Malloy won't have the chance to bother you again."

CJ gasped, her eyes questioning. Was it really over? Was she finally free? "Are you telling me that I can come out of protective custody?"

"Kind of." Doug motioned to the living room. "Let's sit down and we can talk about our options."

CJ followed Matt to the couch and curled up next to him as Doug gave them the basic details of what had happened to Malloy. He went on to explain that most of Rush's funds had been seized at the time he was arrested, but they were still tracking down the money transfers that had paid for the last set of assassins, the ones that had shot CJ's double at the LA swim meet.

Once the government discovered where that money had come from, the belief was that Rush would be incapable of retaliation even if he wanted it. Now that he had been found guilty, CJ's death served no useful purpose except to exact revenge. Since Rush was in prison for the rest of his life, once the last of his money was seized, his ability to harm her would be significantly reduced. She supposed her life might never be quite normal, but finally she at least had the possibility of something close to normal.

"So that's it?" CJ asked. "All of a sudden I am just like everyone else again?"

"Not exactly," Doug replied. "We already have someone working on consolidating your meet results so that they will all be under one name for the Olympic trials. You can continue to use an alias, or you can use your name. It's up to you." Doug didn't give her a chance to voice her preference before he continued on. "Either way, Tara and Lacey will provide security for you at the trials and at the Olympics. If I have my way, I'll be tagging along too."

CJ looked hopefully at Tara and Lacey. "Does that mean you're going to stay here until after the Olympics?"

Lacey shook his head. "Just Tara. I'll be heading out to do the advance work for the trials."

"I'll stick around until they seize the rest of Rush's funds and until we confirm that Malloy is dead," Tara explained. "Then I'll fly out with you and Pete to Long Beach, where we'll meet up with Lacey."

As though he had heard his name, Pete opened the back door, his eyes sweeping the room until they landed on Lacey. "It's one thing to get roped into helping, and another to be the only one working while you all lollygag around."

"I guess that means we'd better get back to work." Tara laughed and pushed up from her chair, eyeing Lacey. "I'll help CJ put away her kitchen stuff. You guys can go finish unloading the boxes."

"The women have spoken," Doug muttered, nodding his head toward the front door.

Tara waited until the men had left the room. "Well, that was easy." She looked over at the stacks of boxes. "Now let's get this stuff put away so you can start enjoying your new kitchen."

"I like the way you think," CJ said, grinning.

She wanted to go see what Matt was doing, but she forced herself to concentrate on the kitchen. Still, in between tasks, her mind raced over the news of the past half hour. Just when she thought she might never regain control of her life, almost everything she had dreamed of was handed to her all at once. In just another week, she would be at the Olympic trials trying to make the rest of her dreams come true.

CJ and Tara were just putting away the last of the dishes when Pete walked into the kitchen.

"You had better eat something and get ready for practice," Pete ordered, looking at CJ.

CJ glanced at her watch, surprised to see that it was already after eleven. "I'm just going to make a sandwich." She looked from Pete to Tara. "Do either of you want one?"

Pete stared at her for a moment, apparently considering her offer. "Tell you what. If you make me lunch, I might consider letting you practice here this afternoon."

"Go for the chicken salad," Tara suggested, already pulling ingredients out of the refrigerator.

CJ looked over at her and motioned at the groceries Tara had lined up on the counter. "Are you going to help, or do you want to go see who else is hungry?"

"I'll check on the guys."

CJ laughed as Tara quickly deserted the kitchen. She turned to Pete and asked, "Are you serious? Can I practice here today?"

"It won't hurt you for one practice." Pete slid onto a stool by the breakfast bar. "That should give you a little more time to get unpacked before we go back over to the University tonight."

"Thanks, Pete."

"Yeah, well, you're still short."

* * *

Matt rolled over in bed, his stomach grumbling from neglect. The blackout blinds he had installed the day before kept the room dark and hid any evidence of whether it was day or night. Swinging his feet over the side of the bed, he rubbed his hands over his face and wondered what day it was. He debated briefly whether he should grab a shower or breakfast first. Breakfast won. Still in his pajamas, he stumbled down the hallway toward the light. He was halfway down the stairs when he smelled something good . . . something baking.

Assuming CJ's habits hadn't changed much over the past few months, he figured it must be the weekend. CJ almost always spent her Saturdays experimenting in the kitchen. He breathed deeply and lengthened his stride. She was baking something blueberry.

The kitchen counters were cluttered with cooking ingredients and mixing bowls. One bowl rested near the stove, a towel covering it. Something simmered on the stove, scenting the air with cinnamon, but Matt honed in on the cooling rack laden with blueberry scones.

CJ stepped out from behind the refrigerator door, a milk jug in one hand. She reached into the cabinet next to it and pulled out a glass. Spotting Matt, she pulled out a second glass. "Hungry?"

"Mmmm." Matt gave her a quick kiss and plucked a scone from the rack. He took another look around, remembering that CJ was leaving tonight for the Olympic trials. "Why are you cooking? Shouldn't you be getting ready?"

"I'm too nervous," CJ explained. "I thought this morning's practice would help me work out the nerves, but I just can't stop thinking about what might happen the next few days."

"You'll be great," Matt assured her. "I just wish my manager would let me take a few days off so I could be there the whole time."

"You've only been with your team a few weeks. I think it's a bit early to be asking for favors."

Matt shrugged, taking a bite of his scone. Furrowing his brow, he turned to his wife and held up the half-eaten scone. "You know, I'm not sure these taste quite right."

"Oh, really?" CJ raised an eyebrow suspiciously as Matt popped the rest of his scone into his mouth.

Matt nodded, struggling to keep a serious face as he used his long reach to snatch another scone from the rack. Playfully, he added, "I'd better test another one, just to be sure."

"I see." CJ fought back a grin. She took a sip of her milk and handed the other glass to Matt.

Matt gulped down a half glass of milk before he noticed that CJ was also drinking milk. "I don't think I've ever seen you drink milk before."

"The nutritionist Pete consulted decided that I'm not getting enough calcium." CJ took another sip, wrinkled her nose, and set her glass on the counter. "I think I'll stick with yogurt."

"What does he think about blueberry scones for breakfast?"

"I could tell you that they're a lot more nutritious than you think they are, but that might ruin it for you." CJ smiled.

"I wouldn't believe you anyway." Matt glanced at his watch and stood up. "I'd better go grab a shower. What time do you fly out tonight?"

"Seven." CJ closed the distance between them and reached up for a kiss. "I'll call you when I get there."

"You'd better." Matt took one step toward the hall before turning back and snatching another scone. He flashed a grin at CJ. "Energy food."

"Right," CJ laughed.

CHAPTER 24

"Pete, you can't be serious." CJ paced across her hotel room. Nationals were just a day away, and he wanted her to scratch out of her first event. "I thought you said I have a good chance of making the Olympic team in the 400 IM."

"You probably can make the Olympic team in the 400, but you won't medal." Pete tapped the papers spread out in front of him on the table in CJ's room. "Besides the fact that I don't want you to get tired out for your 100 breaststroke on Tuesday, the 400 IM is the only race you're trying for that is not a sprint. When we get to the Olympics, I can't properly taper you for both your sprints and a middle distance event."

"Are you sure about this?" CJ asked skeptically.

"Trust me," Pete answered. "I know what I'm doing."

"Okay." CJ motioned toward the door. "Are you sure you don't want to come with me?"

"You're really going to church today? The day before nationals?" Pete shook his head. "I thought you were going to take this Sunday literally as a day of rest."

"Believe me, I am not going to step up in front of everyone for the first time as CJ Whitmore and not do some praying about it first."

Pete narrowed his eyes as he studied her. "Are you sure they won't lynch me because I'm Catholic or Baptist or something?"

"You don't know what religion you are?"

Pete shrugged. "I'm sure I could look it up if I wanted to."

"Come on Pete." CJ opened the door. "Even if you don't believe in modern-day prophets, you can still pray with me."

"All right," Pete grumbled and followed her out the door. "But I'm counting on you to make sure I come out in one piece."

* * *

This was it. CJ took a deep breath and paraded out to the pool with the rest of the finalists for the 100-meter breaststroke. She had competed that morning in the preliminaries for the 200-meter individual medley, advancing to the semifinals that would be held the next day. For now, her focus was on the breaststroke. Bridget Bannon was the top seed in the event. CJ was seeded third, but she considered herself lucky that she was in the lane next to Bridget.

I've beaten her before, CJ reminded herself. If she could beat Bridget, she would make the Olympic team. She already knew it was going to be a close race, and she was trying not to think about the fact that the other swimmers were coming in rested for this meet while CJ would not start her taper until next week to prepare for the Olympics.

She shook her arms, unable to stand still as the adrenaline flowed through her body. For the first time in years, she could feel the support of her loved ones. Matt was in the stands, taking advantage of his one day off this week. Doug and Jill were there to cheer her on as well. A warmth pierced through the excitement of the moment, and she could feel the love of her father and Chase as well. Although both had passed away, she knew their spirits were near.

CJ turned and looked behind her, almost expecting to see her father. Instead, Tara stood behind CJ's block, watching the crowd. Lacey was on the other side of the pool, observing from a different vantage point. The last of Rush's funds had been seized, finally giving CJ something she had dreamed of for years: freedom.

The water rippled gently in front of her, waiting for dreams to be made and others to be broken. The whistle blew and CJ stepped up onto the block. She was ready, and finally she was safe.

All of her insecurities were battled and beaten as she took her position. She sprang forward on the start, hitting the water the same time as her competition. Bridget's height gave her a lead off of the start, but CJ didn't even look at her.

Bridget swam a full body-length ahead of CJ through the first turn and into the second lap. At the sixty-five meter mark, CJ gradually began to close the distance between them. The height advantage that Bridget had on the start and the turn began to dissipate as they approached the finish. As they hit the last ten meters, CJ pushed past Bridget and took the lead for the first time.

The cheering was deafening, but CJ didn't hear it. Her focus was on the timing pad in front of her, the swimmer's equivalent of a finish line. She was swimming her favorite stroke against some of the best competitors in the world. Even as she passed under the flags for her final stroke, she knew she was living the first leg of her childhood dream.

* * *

"This house is incredible." Jill turned a circle in the middle of CJ's kitchen before turning to look at her friend, who leaned against the kitchen counter. "And I can't believe you're actually going to the Olympics."

"*We're* going to the Olympics," CJ corrected. "I thought Doug was inspired to bring you along as part of your honeymoon."

"I can't say I really minded the change in plans," Jill admitted. "Now instead of a week in the Bahamas, I get to spend a week there, a week putting my house together, and another week at the Olympics." Jill sat down at the breakfast bar and shook her head. "I just can't believe I'm getting married this weekend."

"I can't believe you are so calm just three days before your wedding." CJ shook her head as she moved to the refrigerator. She was pleased to see that Matt hadn't depleted their entire supply of water bottles, and then she smiled ironically as she realized it was only because he had been out of town for the past three days. "I was a nervous wreck before Matt and I got married."

"I'm not planning on having armed men chase me to the temple," Jill pointed out.

"Okay, good point." CJ laughed. She opened a bottle of water and handed another one to Jill. "Still, I thought you would have to stay in Dallas to get ready."

"Everything is done," Jill stated. "My mom has organized enough weddings that she has everything down. Besides, I really wanted to be here when we closed on our house."

"I'm so glad you're moving here." CJ set her water bottle on the counter and looked up at Jill. "This all feels so normal. I mean, I think this is what normal is supposed to feel like."

"It's pretty close." Jill glanced at her watch. "I wonder what's keeping Doug. I was hoping to swing by and look at the house before it got dark."

"Matt's flight was probably running late. Doug was going to pick him up from the airport on his way over here," CJ explained. "Did you want the grand tour of my house?"

"That would be great." Jill nodded. "By the way, what happened to Tara? I thought she was still staying here with you."

"She left right before you got here. She has some kind of meeting this evening about my security at the Olympics. Doug figured that since he was headed over here anyway, now was as good a time as any for her to take care of it."

When CJ headed for a pantry rather than the main hall, Jill asked, "Where are you going?"

"Shortcut." CJ motioned for Jill to follow.

Jill followed her into the closeted stairwell. "I never would have known this was here," Jill declared. She pointed at the baseball bat that was perched in the corner next to the door leading to the garage. "I guess Matt's found it already."

"He was supposed to put that in the garage. I found another one in the backyard yesterday." CJ shook her head, thinking how nice it was to have his stuff to clutter up the house again.

CJ showed Jill the rooms near the stairwell. "We haven't really done anything with those rooms yet. I'm not sure what to do with the office they used for all of the security equipment." She pointed to the office that had been converted into a security center. Had she stepped inside, she could have seen various views of the yard and entryway. She shrugged as she headed down the hall toward her room. "I mean, I doubt we need such an extensive security system now."

"It can't hurt to keep it as it is for a while longer. After all, you are married to a celebrity. With the way everyone was talking about you at the trials, you're making quite a name for yourself, too."

"I don't know about that." CJ proceeded to show Jill her room, as well as the room Tara was still staying in. Finally, they ended up back in the kitchen.

"Did you want to put your things in one of the guest rooms?"

"Sure," Jill said, picking up her suitcase and following CJ to the downstairs guest rooms.

"You have a choice between these two," CJ explained.

"This is great." Jill moved into the first room and dropped her suitcase on the bed. "By the way, I found some of your things when I was packing."

CJ watched as Jill opened her bag and pulled out one of CJ's old sweatshirts and the stuffed dolphin CJ had thought was lost long ago. She stared at it with disbelief.

"Where did you find that?" CJ asked incredulously, pointing to the stuffed animal.

"It was under one of the beds." Jill handed it to her. "I think it probably ended up there the day our apartment was ransacked."

CJ ran a hand over the stuffed animal, tears threatening. "I was holding this when Chase was killed. I thought it was lost forever." Remembering her conversation with Doug, she looked up at Jill and declared, "I need to find some scissors."

"What?" Jill followed CJ down the hall into the kitchen and watched CJ pull a pair of scissors out of a drawer. "What are you doing?"

"The men that killed Chase were looking for diamonds the night that they came to his apartment. No one ever found them." Carefully, CJ snipped the seam on the toy dolphin and began pulling the thread free. Then she pushed her finger into the two-inch-wide opening she had created, probing the stuffing. "This is the only thing that was there that night that was never searched."

"You can't think that someone hid diamonds inside . . ." Jill's voice trailed off as CJ began pulling the stuffing out. "Did you find something?"

"It feels like plastic." CJ kept working her fingers around the inside of the toy, finally pulling some stuffing and a plastic bag out of its middle. She cleared away the stuffing, her eyes widening. Lying before her was a thick plastic bag, half filled with glittering stones.

"Are those really diamonds?" Jill moved over to take a closer look.

"I think so." CJ nodded in amazement. "They were right here all along."

Jill flipped open her cell phone. "I'll call Doug."

CJ listened to Jill's side of the conversation while she stared at the diamonds.

"He said they're on their way," Jill stated as she closed her cell phone.

"Did he say how long it will be before he gets here?"

Jill shook her head. "I didn't even think to ask."

CJ picked up the diamonds. "I guess I should stash these somewhere until Doug shows up."

"What are you going to do with them?" Jill asked.

"I don't know." CJ considered the lives affected by the stones in her hand. Looking around the kitchen, she noted that the countertops were clear except for the toaster and a basket of muffins. Earlier that day, Matt had sent CJ the muffin basket, along with a card letting her know he was thinking about her. She smiled as she recalled the sweet words he had written.

Cradling the diamond-filled bag in her hands, CJ wondered where she could store it temporarily. Suddenly, the fire alarms beeped and the lights went out. Pulling open the nearest kitchen drawer, CJ dropped the diamonds inside. "It looks like I'm not going to be cooking dinner tonight."

"Hopefully the power won't be off for that long," Jill commented.

"Just in case, I'd better go find a flashlight." CJ nodded at the window overlooking the backyard. "It's going to be dark before much longer."

"Do you have any candles?" Jill asked as CJ started toward the main hall.

"Look in the cabinet next to the stove," CJ answered. "I'll be right back."

CJ turned the corner into the front entryway, evening shadows making the hall darker than she expected. Her footsteps quickened as she anxiously headed for the table in the entryway where she remembered storing a flashlight. As she leaned over to open the table's single drawer, she heard a sound in the dining room, and her hands flew to her heart. She whipped around to face the sound, realizing that someone else was in the house. An instant later, her jaw dropped open as she saw a gun aimed at her chest.

"Hello, Christal."

CJ forced her eyes away from the handgun, lifting them to the face of the man who held it, a man who was supposed to be dead. *This can't be right,* she thought. But it was indeed Jimmy Malloy standing in her dining room. CJ's heart pounded, disbelief and confusion almost overcoming her.

He moved forward and looked around the entryway casually as though he was an invited guest or a good friend who just happened to stop by for a visit. His voice sounded sincere when he schooled his eyes back on CJ. "You have a nice house here. Quiet, isolated." He paused and gave her a pointed look. "Safe."

CJ couldn't speak. This murderous man had somehow gained access to her house, and all she could do was stare. She hadn't even screamed. He waved the gun in her direction, motioning for her to step back down the hall. Seeing the gun once more, she decided that maybe screaming wouldn't have done any good anyway. She tried to take a deep breath to find her voice and found that even breathing was becoming a struggle.

"What do you want?" CJ finally gasped, her voice barely audible.

"A great many things." Malloy stepped farther into the house, a slow smile crossing his face as CJ automatically took a step back.

CJ swallowed hard. Malloy's eyes were dark and cold as they bore into hers. She had no doubt that this man had killed before, and instinct told her that he planned on killing again. Her life held no value to him, but still her brain clouded with questions. Why now? What would he gain by killing her now? If everyone thought he was dead, she was no longer a threat to him.

"To start with, I want to know where those diamonds are."

"Diamonds?" CJ's eyes widened, and the confusion she felt from his presence showed on her face. Fear paralyzed her, even as a corner of her brain wondered how he could know that she had discovered the stones. Out of the corner of her eye, CJ saw movement. Jill!

Malloy swung the gun toward Jill now. Without thought, CJ stepped between them. "Don't hurt her. She's doesn't know anything."

Malloy's eyes met hers, his intentions clear. "She's seen me."

"Please," CJ tried again. "I'll help you find the diamonds."

"You stupid girl," Malloy retorted scornfully. He pulled a photograph out of his pocket. "You've had them all along."

CJ forced herself to look at the photograph, surprised to see herself with her old roommates. She was holding a stuffed teddy bear that Jill had given her for Christmas.

"What are you talking about?" CJ managed, fear tinting her voice.

"I know you took a stuffed animal from the cop's house the day he was killed. That has to be where he hid the diamonds."

CJ almost headed for the kitchen, hoping that if she gave Malloy what he wanted, he would spare their lives. The hardness in his eyes told her that negotiating with him would never work. Her disbelief and terror subsided just long enough for her to consider her options. She could barely think over the pounding of her heart, but she knew they had to find a way to warn Matt and Doug and call for help.

CJ backed up until she was right in front of Jill. She reached back and took Jill's hand, feeling it tremble and knowing her own hand shook as well. "We'll go find it for you."

"Oh, no." Malloy laughed again. "I'm not letting you out of my sight." He pointed the gun at Jill once more, noticing the cell phone in her hand. "First, give me that phone. Then she can go get it."

Still keeping her body between them, CJ reached back and took the phone from Jill. She handed it to Malloy, silently praying that Jill would find a way to get out of the house and call for help.

"While you're at it," Malloy barked, glaring at CJ, "give me your cell phone too."

CJ complied, retrieving her phone from her pocket and handing it to him. Then she said to Jill, "Go into the bedroom and find the teddy bear. I think it's in the closet."

Jill stared at the gun in Malloy's hand, apparently unable to move.

"Please, Jill," CJ croaked, emotion clogging her voice. The image of Chase staring down the two men that killed him flashed vividly in her mind. He had saved her life; now she could only hope she could do the same for Jill. CJ could almost hear Chase's voice as she touched Jill's shoulder and formed the words, "Go into the bedroom."

Slowly, tentatively, Jill moved toward the stairway. Once she reached the top of the stairs, her footsteps sounded as she raced the length of the hall.

As a door slammed, CJ turned to face Malloy again and wondered how long he would wait.

CHAPTER 25

Jill's whole body trembled as she picked up the telephone in the office, shocked when there was no dial tone. It took her a minute to remember that the cordless phone wouldn't work without electricity. She searched the alarm panel next to the bank of monitors and found the button to signal the silent alarm. She pushed it right before noticing that the indicator light was off, signaling that the system wasn't functioning. For the first time, she looked over at the monitors to see that they were all blank.

Terrified, she closed her eyes and uttered a simple prayer. "Father, please help me." She wasn't even sure what help she needed, nor could her mind wrap around the possibilities. She wanted to live. Never before had she been faced with such a drastic demonstration of the alternative, but she desperately wanted her life to continue, and she wanted it to go on with Doug safely at her side.

She couldn't begin to imagine what CJ was going through, but she had lived with her old roommate long enough to know that she would be thinking of Matt's safety right now as much as her own. Surely there was a way to get a message to Doug and Matt. She couldn't let them arrive unaware of the danger waiting for them, and maybe, just maybe, they could help her and CJ get away from the terrifying man downstairs.

Jill looked out the window, unable to see any indication of how Malloy had arrived or if anyone was with him. She noticed the boat tied to the dock and turned away from the window. If she could get to the boat . . .

Crossing the hall, Jill opened the door to the hidden stairwell and quietly climbed down to the bottom. She opened the door leading to the garage and looked around. She crossed to the far side of the garage, finding the door leading into the backyard.

Stepping outside, she kept her body against the wall so that she wouldn't be visible through the living room windows. She surveyed the yard, calculating how she could make it to the dock without being seen from the house.

Thinking of her many games of hide-and-seek growing up, Jill stepped into the shrubbery along the wall between CJ's house and the one next door. She heard movement in the front yard, and hid just as a man came through the gate on the far side of the backyard. Quietly, she moved deeper behind a shrub and listened as the man circled the yard. He stopped just a few feet from her, and Jill was afraid he could hear the pounding of her heart. Finally, he moved back toward the other side of the yard, and her fear lessened slightly.

She breathed a sigh of relief when she heard the unidentified man move back into the front yard. Carefully, she scooted along the wall, hiding behind palm trees and greenery. Finally, she came to the water's edge and wondered how she would make it across the yard to the boat.

Realizing that she would be completely exposed to the house if she ran across the yard, Jill squatted down and slipped into the water. She swam to the dock, then alongside of it until she reached the boat. With a prayer in her heart, she grabbed the top rung of the short ladder on the back of the boat.

Silently, she counted to three and then swung herself up into the boat and dropped down onto the deck. Staying on her hands and knees, she moved to the front of the boat and found just what she was looking for. Less than a minute later, she had the Coast Guard on the radio, and her fingers trembled around the gun she had found in the glove box.

* * *

His heart racing, Doug made the call for back-up. His tires squealed as he took a corner too fast, but his voice remained steady as he relayed the address to the local police and proceeded to provide details.

"Our suspect is armed and dangerous and has at least one hostage." Doug's stomach knotted as he considered that CJ might not be the only one in danger. He couldn't even consider the possibility that the woman he was going to marry in just a few days could be in peril. He didn't know if he could remain levelheaded if he thought about it, so he clung to the hope that Jill would stay hidden.

Doug didn't dare look at Matt, seated on the passenger side of the car. He had already warned Matt that he had to stay out of sight when they got to the house, and he could only hope Matt would listen. Since Matt wasn't trained to deal with armed criminals—and since he would do anything for CJ—he might be reckless and do something to endanger them all.

Doug cut off a van as he swerved through downtown traffic. He ignored the annoyed gesture from the other driver, praying that he wasn't too late.

* * *

"What's taking her so long?" Malloy asked impatiently as he paced across the living room to the hall.

CJ started to make excuses, but one glance at Malloy's face changed her mind. He looked like a caged animal, edgily pacing back and forth. Terrified, CJ watched Malloy look down the hall and then turn back to her, his right hand gripping his gun tighter and his eyes narrowing as he checked his watch. His cockiness had subsided over the past few minutes, agitation rapidly replacing it. CJ could sense him losing control, and she was beginning to think she liked the cocky version of Malloy over the frustrated man pacing in front of her.

Tension vibrated through the room, and CJ tried to ignore the throbbing in her temples and the nausea settling in her stomach. More than once she wondered if she could just be having a bad dream. Malloy was supposed to be dead—he couldn't really be here. She was supposed to be safe now.

So many times she had feared for her life. Over and over again she had faced the threats, the danger, the countless people who had wanted her dead. Each time the Lord had spared her life. Could she really have come this far only to have it end like this? Never before had she been so afraid, so helpless, and she knew she couldn't survive the day alone. Her mind raced, variations of the same words running over and over in her head. *Please, Father, let me get out of this alive. Please keep Matt and Jill and Doug safe.*

CJ sucked in her breath when Malloy turned to her again, closing the distance between them. With a wave of his gun, he grabbed her arm. "Come on."

CJ's body went rigid at his touch, another wave of nausea hitting her hard. Malloy tightened his grip on her arm, pulling her toward the stairs. She stumbled, but Malloy continued forward. "I'm tired of waiting. I know those diamonds are here."

"My closet was a mess. She probably couldn't find it," she stuttered, hoping to stall him.

Malloy shoved CJ in front of him, and they made their way up the stairs and approached the bedroom door. "Open it."

CJ moved as slowly as she could while still trying to look natural. *She should be safe by now,* she thought. Nearly five minutes had passed since Jill had disappeared into the bedroom. As long as Jill remembered which door led to the hidden stairway, she should have had plenty of time to get out and make her way through the garage.

Now if she could just stall Malloy until help arrived. CJ blinked back the tears that formed in her eyes. She tried to push aside the realization that the man behind her had every intention of killing her.

The moment CJ turned the doorknob, Malloy pushed the door open and shoved her into the bedroom. He walked around the empty room, and then moved to the bathroom and the closet. He looked inside and then trained the gun on CJ again. "Where is she?"

"I don't know." CJ's eyes darted to the bedroom door. If she ran, would he shoot her? Or was she better off trying to stall him in hopes that help would arrive soon?

"Where is she?" Malloy repeated. As he looked at CJ, pure evil exuded from him. His jaw clenched as he grabbed her hair, pulling her closer to him. A scream pierced the air, one of shock and fear. Her scream. CJ trembled, breathing rapidly as complete terror took over her psyche. As he pressed the gun to CJ's temple, Malloy spoke in a deep, even tone. "I'm going to ask you one last time. Where are the diamonds?"

CJ gasped for breath, barely able to form words. "I hid them." She faltered, waving in the general direction of the bedroom door. "Downstairs."

She could feel the cold steel of the gun barrel against her skin, her pulse increasing beneath it. Malloy's hand clenched her hair tighter and she bit back another scream. She could almost hear him considering if he should just shoot her now and find the diamonds himself.

"You won't find them without me," CJ said quickly. "I'll get them for you."

"No more stalling." Malloy's voice was clipped and impatient.

His hand still fisted in her hair, Malloy pulled CJ back toward the stairs as she wondered if help would ever arrive.

* * *

Matt clenched and unclenched his hands as Doug drove as quickly as traffic would allow. They were passing the beach near his and CJ's new house when they turned the corner to find a wall of cars blocking the street.

"This can't be happening!" Matt looked at Doug desperately. He didn't want to think about the danger CJ was in, but he couldn't think of anything else. Each minute, each second that passed by might make the difference of whether she lived or died. He blinked hard as he felt his eyes water at the thought of life without her. He couldn't accept that idea—wouldn't accept it.

"The police should already be there by now," Doug offered, lifting his cell phone to his ear.

His body already vibrating with adrenaline, Matt saw the look on Doug's face as he listened to the person on the other end, and it did nothing to calm Matt down. He felt like everything was closing in on him, and he wanted to just get out and start running. They were still a couple of miles away from CJ, and there was no way to be sure if they went on foot they would get there faster.

Doug flipped the phone closed, cranked the wheel, and forced the car to jump the embankment to the other side of the street. "There's an accident blocking the entrance to your neighborhood."

"What aren't you telling me?" Matt asked as Doug pulled the car into a parking lot next to the marina.

"A cement truck didn't hear the sirens and ran through the intersection just as two police cars were turning into your neighborhood. The cops aren't in the greatest shape, and none of their buddies is going to make it to your house anytime soon with the road blocked," Doug explained. "All of the Coast Guard boats in the area responded to a bad boat wreck, and it's going to be at least ten minutes before any of them get there."

The car screeched to a stop at the marina. Instinctively, Matt scrambled out and followed Doug onto the long wooden dock. Boats swayed gently in the current, only a few people in sight on the quiet weekday afternoon. To their right a good-sized yacht was occupied by an elderly couple sitting on the deck. Without a second glance, Doug made a beeline for a man walking toward them. The man was long and lean, probably in his late thirties, and he bore a classic anchor tattoo on his arm. To Matt, the man's flat-top haircut and the tattoo suggested he had been a Navy man.

Doug raised a hand in greeting as they approached. "Hey, is one of these boats yours?"

"Yeah, that one." The man pointed at a speed boat, beaming with pride. "She isn't that big, but she's fast."

"Great. I need to borrow it."

The man stepped back, pure shock on his face. "What?"

Doug flashed his badge as he spoke. "It's a police emergency." He dug out a business card and handed it to him.

"You've got to be kidding me."

Matt stepped forward, impatience simmering. "He isn't kidding. It's a matter of life and death."

"Look, I'd be happy to help you, but I just redid the steering controls. It'll take a few minutes to show you how to operate the boat," the man told him. Seeing the frustration radiating from Doug and Matt, he added, "I'll be happy to take you wherever you want to go."

"You've got to be kidding." Doug shook his head impatiently.

The man just shrugged and shook his head.

Matt knew Doug was at the end of his rope. With a deep breath, he laid a hand on Doug's arm. "Doug, we don't have time to waste."

Doug's teeth were clenched as he nodded to the boat. "Let's go, but you both had better keep your heads down."

Thirty seconds later Doug and Matt were on the boat and headed out to sea with Butch, a former Navy mechanic who now made his living repairing yachts. He just nodded casually when Doug told him where they were going.

By the time Butch turned the boat into the channel leading into Matt's neighborhood, Doug was already on the radio trying to contact Jill. With a little help from the Coast Guard, he finally found the right frequency.

Doug's rigid stance relaxed slightly when Jill's voice came over the radio in a hushed tone.

"Doug?" she whispered. "Be careful. There's someone in the backyard."

Aware that they were on an open frequency, Doug kept his response brief. "Just stay down. I'll take care of it."

"Please hurry," Jill started. Suddenly, she shrieked and a gunshot sounded. The radio dropped out of Doug's hand, swinging by its cord as the connection was lost.

CHAPTER 26

CJ yelped with pain as Malloy yanked on her hair to force her down the stairs. Just as they reached the landing, she heard a gunshot outside. Her heart sank as she thought about Jill and the possibility of Matt and Doug arriving as well.

Malloy let out a distorted laugh. "Sounds like my associate located your friend."

She gasped for air, guilt overwhelming her as she thought of Jill possibly being injured—or worse—because of her. CJ's legs and arms felt like jelly, her body moving forward only because Malloy continued to drag her with him. A second gunshot sounded.

Think, CJ ordered herself. Help should have been here by now.

Her eyes landed on the coat closet, and she knew that she had to at least try to get away. She might still be able to help whomever Malloy's thug was shooting at outside. "I hid the diamonds in one of the guest rooms," CJ ventured, pointing down the hall.

Malloy released her hair and gave her a shove into the hall in front of him. "Which one?"

"This one." CJ walked through the bedroom's open door ahead of him. "In the back of the closet."

"Get them," he growled, making a point to train the gun on her.

She pulled open the door and stepped into the closet. She squatted down, grateful that some of Matt's things cluttered the floor so she could give the appearance of searching. Edging deeper into the closet, CJ glanced back to see that Malloy was still standing near the middle of the bedroom.

With a silent prayer and a rush of adrenaline, she reached up, wrapped her fingers around the doorknob of the adjoining closet, and burst out into the hallway. She sprinted toward the kitchen with her eyes focused on the door leading to the garage. The shout behind her didn't slow her down, nor did the approaching footsteps. Then a gunshot echoed through the house and stopped her cold.

* * *

Matt stepped forward and gripped the side of the boat with both hands as they turned the corner near his and CJ's house. No one had moved for a few seconds after they heard the gunshot through the radio, then Doug had leaned over and increased the boat's speed himself, ignoring Butch's annoyed stare.

The house came into view even as Matt tried to focus on what they could do to save CJ and Jill. The dock near the house was in full view from the windows on the back of the house. "Doug, they're going to see us coming."

Doug nodded. "Which is why we're going to pull up to the dock next door." He pointed at the little dock that belonged to Matt's next-door neighbor.

Butch cut the boat's speed and turned the wheel to edge in where Doug had indicated. "Do you want me to wait for you?"

Doug started to say no, but movement in the yard caught his eye. Before he could respond, Butch tied off the boat with a single line. With a nod of approval, Doug drew his weapon and turned to Matt. "I want you to stay here with Butch."

"You know better than that," Matt answered as another gunshot vibrated through the quiet neighborhood.

Matt leaped from the boat and sprinted along the neighbor's yard toward his own. Doug sent Butch a look and ordered him to stay down before Doug jumped up to follow Matt. Both men slowed briefly to scale the wrought-iron fence that separated the two yards, and before Doug could stop him, Matt headed straight across the open yard for the back door.

Hearing movement behind him, Doug turned back toward the water. His jaw dropped when he saw Jill standing in the boat, holding a gun with both hands. In his surprise and relief, he didn't notice the movement in the bushes along the wall. Matt had only taken six or seven steps when Jill shot across the yard to help ward off the threat that Doug and Matt had yet to see.

Another gunshot sounded at the same time, but Matt never broke stride. Doug immediately switched back to cop mode and aimed his weapon toward the bushes. He squeezed off a round to cover Matt, shouting at Jill to get down.

She didn't have to be told twice.

* * *

CJ barely had time to blink as Malloy lunged toward her. She had dropped to the floor when a bullet splintered the garage door she had been attempting to open. Shaking, she tried to get her feet underneath her so she could stand, but all she managed to do was push herself along the floor until her back was up against the wall.

Malloy reached down and squeezed one hand around her throat. "You stupid girl!"

CJ grabbed his arm with both of her hands and opened her mouth in an attempt to breathe. As his fingers squeezed tighter, her eyes grew huge with panic, her pulse racing.

Suddenly, Malloy loosened his hold just enough for her to gasp for air. "Now, are you ready to cooperate?"

CJ nodded emphatically, and Malloy released his grip on her throat.

"The diamonds are here, in the kitchen."

"Where?"

"In one of the drawers." CJ slowly pulled herself up, her breathing quick and shallow. Fear consumed her—fear for her life, for her husband, and for her friends. The scene almost seemed unreal, as though she was watching a television show—a show about someone else. Still a little dazed, CJ opened one drawer to find the diamonds weren't there. "It was one of these over here." She slid open a second drawer and looked down at the bag of diamonds inside.

He's going to kill me, she thought now. *As soon as he sees them, he's going to kill me.*

She didn't notice the sound at the door as she reached into the drawer. In a sudden move, she grabbed the bag of gems and hurled it at Malloy. The sudden motion caught him off guard, giving CJ a chance to dart toward the door. Before she could reach it, Matt burst through it. He swung a baseball bat with all of his might, a look of utter fury on his face. The bat connected with Malloy's shoulder, knocking him forward as he cried out in pain.

The diamonds dropped to the floor and Malloy's gun clattered onto the kitchen counter. Malloy reached for it, his fingers wrapping around the handle just as Matt dropped the baseball bat and grabbed him from behind. The gun tumbled out of sight onto one of the kitchen stools as Malloy twisted free and turned to face Matt.

Malloy's eyes glinted with challenge, and he glanced at CJ, who was now trapped in the corner of the kitchen. He then looked back to Matt, apparently pleased that CJ couldn't get out of the kitchen without getting by him. "Even if you get past me, my friend outside isn't going to let you out of here alive."

A burst of gunfire sounded, and Matt gave a satisfied nod toward the wall of windows overlooking the backyard. Had any of them looked through the window, they would have seen Doug leaning over Malloy's accomplice to verify that he no longer had a pulse. "It sounds like your friend is having his own trouble."

"Or yours are," Malloy retorted right before lunging at Matt.

Matt's head snapped back when Malloy's fist connected with his jaw, but Malloy didn't keep the upper hand for long. Matt managed a clear punch to Malloy's midsection, causing him to fall back against the kitchen counter.

CJ looked down at the baseball bat on the floor, wondering if she could get to it as Malloy and Matt continued their fistfight. When Malloy fell to the floor, he grabbed the bat and held it out to keep Matt at bay.

Realizing that Malloy was trying to get to the other side of the counter to retrieve his gun, CJ climbed onto the counter and then dropped onto one of the kitchen stools. Just then, Malloy took a swing at Matt with the bat, clearing the edge of the counter.

CJ looked down on the floor, and when she couldn't see the gun there, she started looking on the stools. She saw the gun just as Malloy lunged for it.

"Run, Matt!" CJ shouted.

Malloy's hand grasped the gun, and he aimed it at CJ as she tried to scramble past him. A gunshot sounded, CJ screamed, and Malloy crumpled to the floor.

CJ looked up to see Doug standing beside Matt.

"Are you okay?" Matt asked breathlessly.

Speechless, CJ started to cry as Matt moved forward and pulled her into his arms. Her whole body shook as Doug stepped on Malloy's hand, removed the gun, and checked for a pulse.

"Is he . . . ?" CJ managed to ask, unaware of Jill running across the backyard toward the house.

Doug nodded, looking up as Jill opened the back door. She saw Doug immediately, then Matt holding CJ in his arms. Jill looked back at Doug before she spoke. "What happened? I heard gunshots in here!"

Doug closed the distance between them and pulled Jill into his arms. He was still stunned that she had engaged in a gunfight with Malloy's accomplice after the man had tried to shoot her. Thankfully, he had hit the boat's radio instead. Doug didn't think he would ever be able to dislodge the image of her shooting at a trained killer. He took a deep breath before finding his voice. "Everything's okay now."

Still stunned, CJ motioned down at Malloy and then looked back up at Jill. "He was going to kill us."

"It's over now," Matt soothed her, pulling her into the living room where she could no longer see Malloy's lifeless form. She looked up at him with a pale face as he reiterated the words. "It's really over."

EPILOGUE

CJ watched the American flag rising as the first notes of the national anthem began to play. She felt the weight of the gold medal around her neck and watched the hand-held flags waving in the stands. Tears burned the back of her eyes as emotions overwhelmed her. She tried to blink back the tears as Kristin Hart put an arm around her shoulder, uniting her with the rest of her team.

This was the third time she had made it to the medal stand. The first had been when she won the silver in the 100-meter breaststroke. Then she had won the bronze in the 200-meter individual medley, surprising even herself. The U.S. national anthem had played then too, since Kristin Hart had won the gold, but it wasn't the same. This time the music played for her and the three teammates she had grown so close to over the past several days. Although they had not been the favorites going into the race, they had beaten some of the best swimmers in the world to capture the gold in the 4-by-100-meter medley relay.

As with all Olympic Games, stories about the athletes filtered to the public as media attention grew—especially stories about medal winners. The stories about CJ that appeared right after the trials had taken on a life of their own, and CJ quickly became one of the faces of the summer

Olympics. Her story had been told and retold so many times that she wondered if anyone *didn't* think of her as "that girl from the Witness Protection Program."

She thought of how much had happened in the past few years and the many detours in her road to the Olympics. Though she had only skimmed a few of the articles written about her, one had brought home a fact she hadn't yet considered. Since Chase's death, seven attempts had been made on her life, and seven times she had survived. The reporter had called her lucky, but CJ knew it was more than that.

She didn't know why the Lord had chosen to spare her life so many times, but now, listening to the national anthem, she could only hope to be worthy of the many blessings that had gotten her here. Throughout the past week, she had felt the support of her friends, her country, and at times, even her father.

When CJ had failed to reach the finals in the 200-meter breaststroke, her disappointment had been keen, not so much because of her own desire to succeed, but rather because she felt she had disappointed an entire country. Despite that failure, the support from her newfound fans never wavered. The stories about CJ's situation had struck a chord with the American public, and their interest in her continued despite her inability to make the medal stand in one of her best events. New opportunities in her career abounded, but CJ already knew where her priorities would lie now. For too long she had put her dreams, and her father's dream, of swimming in the Olympics in front of everything else. Now she knew it was time to let the fame fade away so that she could finally redefine her priorities, with family at the top of the list.

As the final notes of "The Star-Spangled Banner" rang out, CJ's eyes found Matt in the front row a short distance away. As much as she didn't want this moment to end, she could hardly wait for the moments still to come. For the rest of her life, she would be able to look back and remember this, the instant her Olympic dreams came true. As Matt's eyes met hers, she knew that this was also just the beginning of many extraordinary days to come.

ABOUT THE AUTHOR

Traci Hunter Abramson is originally from Phoenix, Arizona. After graduating from Brigham Young University, she worked for the Central Intelligence Agency for six years before resigning to become a stay-at-home mom.

Traci currently resides with her husband and four children in Stafford, Virginia, where she serves as the stake young women's sports director. She spends much of her free time writing, reading, and transporting kids to soccer games (usually three at the same time on opposite ends of the county). She also coaches the North Stafford High School swim team. *The Deep End* is her third novel.